SURFACE

By Alex Ritchie

About the Author and Book

I started writing this book as early as 2004 based simply on a vivid dream I had one night. After writing the first few chapters, my life took on new priorities and I practically forgot about this book for years; however, the narrative never left me. It was not until early 2011, on one of my adventures, that an almost total stranger said out of the blue that I should write a book. This prompted me to continue, I thought, why not? After all, I had some genuinely good ideas. So after a further two years hard work of writing and re-writing, this book was born.

I have a normal job, a software developer, so at first glance my life does not seem all that interesting. So you may wonder where do I get my inspiration for this book? Well, you would have to delve deeper into my life and take a look at my life that takes place at the weekend, for I spend each and every weekend exploring the strange world that is beneath our feet, I am a caver, or as some would call me, a potholer.

I have pushed myself hard in this endeavour and have plenty of mishaps and stories to tell, but this book is not about those stories. This book is a fantasy book written by a person who can draw upon lots of real life experiences of things that most would not even dare to try. Quite a few of the places I write about in this book are inspired by

Surface

places I have been and seen, be they above or below ground. However, many of the book's pages come straight out of my imagination.

As for the characters, who are they based on? Me perhaps? I would have to say a little yes, such as Luke's spirit of adventure, but that is where I think the similarities between them and me end. I have deliberately tried not to write myself much into this book, after all it is an exciting process for me evolving the characters as they deal with the situations they find them selves in. What choices would they make? I hope it will be just as exciting for you the reader.

Acknowledgements

My dear parents, Margaret & Steven Ritchie – For their honest feedback and support.
Don Miller – For the final proofreading.
Carla M Jennings – For telling me to write it.
All my caving friends – For giving me the opportunity to get inspiration for this book

Prologue

Luke is being removed, banished if you will, from a society that has taken refuge beneath the earth. This society took refuge below ground after a sudden ice age brought on when the sun began to very slowly die.

For his entire life Luke had lived underground in this society never seeing the sun or the outside, other than what he had seen in pictures and read in books. This would soon change one day shortly after his 23rd birthday.

Despite a comfortable life, Luke always wanted more; he did not consider himself an adrenaline freak, or even a real adventurer, but he just had to strive for the unknown. There was so much he wanted to know, there were so many unanswered questions. So one day after a rather drab 23rd birthday party, he set off for a journey to the upper echelons of his underground world, not knowing what he would find.

It was forbidden to go up there, but why he wondered? It was a long journey just to reach the start. On his last journey he left his post and travelled miles upon miles through the old geothermal steam tunnels. He eventually passed tunnel 4V about three miles away from

Prologue

Geothermal Control. He hoped that the steam pressure remained low today as these tunnels were still used to vent excess pressure. He reached tunnel 4W, which was his destination. At the end of the tunnel lay an old brick wall, a wall that was now collapsing. He had already scouted through here before, but he found that he lacked the proper supplies and equipment to scale the shaft that led up a few hundred meters beyond the broken wall.

Perhaps he had aroused suspicions when he acquired the many ropes and metal bolts he would need, or maybe someone saw him last time, he did not know. The only thing he did know was that this time the Hammerites were waiting for him. He tried to run the way he came, but more Hammerites emerged, blocking off his escape. They pounced upon him and he was quickly restrained, despite his valiant yet pointless struggles.

He was quickly brought up on charges for what used to be considered only a minor crime, a crime of curiosity, officially known as trespassing on forbidden grounds.

The punishment was to be severe. The presiding Hammerite, one F Olsworth, read out the sentence in an official tone: "You are to be taken from this court and shall be banished to the surface, where nothing but the cold embrace of death awaits you". Luke had not even been given the chance to defend himself. As he was dragged away he pleaded that he was only guilty of being curious,

Surface

yet his cries for leniency fell on deaf ears.

Reality hit home, and a shiver ran down Luke's spine as his pulse began to race. He knew that the judge was right, banishment meant death. As far as he knew no one had ever returned from the surface. The books Luke had read described the surface as a dark, freezing hostile place where temperatures of 60 degrees below zero were the norm and howling winds that would strip the warmth from your body in a matter of seconds and leave you dead in a matter of minutes.

Once the hammer of justice fell, it took the Hammerites very little time to bundle Luke into the elevator at the centre of the Hammerite building, an elevator bound for the surface. Two guards joined Luke on the elevator, but they never said a word, regardless of how much Luke protested; "How can you do this to me? Don't you know I will die up there? You know, you are as good as murderers!". The guards just stared at Luke blankly; no emotion was visible on their faces for they wore masks with only their eyes visible. A key was turned and the elevator began to rise at a fair rate.

The elevator took several minutes to reach the surface, but several minutes for a condemned man seem like an eternity. Despite an eternity all too quickly the elevator came to a halt, their journey at an end. The doors slid open. To his surprise they did not emerge into a snow

Prologue

storm, though Luke did notice that the air was noticeably colder. He stepped out and could see they were still indoors, perhaps even still underground. Luke surveyed his surroundings knowing that this sight would be the last thing he would ever see before the white death that lay before him outside. Unfortunately for Luke, his last ever sight would be of bleak decaying concrete that covered the floor, ceiling and walls.

They left the elevator behind and made their way down the corridor before taking a left turn. At this point, Luke noticed a light emanating from somewhere above. It was daylight, though its source, at the top of a small shaft was too far away and the shaft too narrow for Luke to make anything out of the outside. As he crossed the threshold into the light, he felt a cold breeze strike his body and began to shiver preemptively. He froze on the spot knowing what was to come, at least he did until the guards prodded him forwards.

The guards continued to prod Luke along the cold grey corridor until their way was blocked. Ahead a cold steel door sealed the passage with the words "Blast door" embroidered on it in a red font. One of the guards pulled a hefty lever to the side of the door several times, but nothing appeared to happen. "A reprieve"!, Luke thought. But all too soon the door began to slide slowly upwards. The door creaked and protested as it grinded its way up, as if the movement caused it pain. As soon as the door was

Surface

high enough to walk under the guards pushed Luke through into the small chamber beyond. Ahead, twenty feet away, stood an identical door. To Luke's surprise they followed him inside.

"Come to freeze to death with me?", Luke enquired. The guards still did not respond.

Darkness began to enclose the three of them as the door they had just passed through began to lower. A loud crash in the darkness indicated that the door behind them had fully closed and sealed itself. Luke continued to shiver, either through the cold air blowing in from the vents above, or through the fear of knowing that these were the last few moments of his life. Then out of the darkness came the sounds of clicking and clunking as machinery sprang into life. The door in front began to raise.

Luke clutched his shirt tight as the outside light and wind rushed in. It would be moments before the cold would strike him down.

Chapter 1: The Last Ride

Antheria sat at her desk at Geothermal Control, her eyes only occasionally flicking up to glance at the various dials. She had her head buried in a manual on *"Geothermal Flow Control and Its Dynamics"*. At least that is what it would look like if anyone happened to glance in her direction. Inside the cover of the manual was another book that if the cover had not been removed would sport the title *"Laws of the Hammerites; Case Studies"* She was studying this forbidden book intently.

Time passed quickly as she carefully read the passages from the book. All the while she never took her eyes off the book for more than a brief second to glance at the dials, the only other distraction being her long and frizzy brunette hair that often fell in front of her bright blue eyes. Alarms occasionally sounded, but she barely raised an eyebrow. This was not like her, she was normally extremely enthusiastic about her work as her it was not only very important to her, but was necessary for the survival of the underground settlement which had been her home for all of her life. But how could she think about her work now? A complete injustice was about to occur for a man she cared about, cared about far more than she let herself believe she did. He was going to be executed in… "Oh no! In half an hours time!" Her book did not tell her anything useful, but she had to try something.

Surface

Antheria bolted upright quickly and stood up from her seat. She ran to the door of the currently empty control room before stopping at the doorway as her conscious pricked her. "No, I cannot leave this station unmanned", she realised. Quickly she returned to her station and reached for the radio. Calmly, more calmly than she would have thought was possible she dialled the station for Johnny in maintenance and began to speak, "Johnny, I am sorry to do this to you, but I need a favour. I need you to cover for me, there is something I must do."

"This is the third time this week! I am on maintenance duty here, I can't just drop what I am doing for your every beck and call," Johnny replied curtly.

"Johnny, this will be the last time, I promise. It is an utter emergency," she said. Getting frustrated now, with time ticking, she added, "Look, I didn't want to resort to this, I know what you get up to down there, I have seen you on the safety cameras. I know, for example, you take various tools and items to add to your "collection" to do who knows what with. I also know how you have doctored the inventory records to cover it all up, but I just happen to have here, an unaltered duplicate, which, when compared to yours... well let's just say it would raise suspicions." Johnny tried to interrupt but failed as Antheria continued, "I wouldn't want your shift supervisor to see it, or even worse the Hammerites, which could

Chapter 1: The Last Ride

happen if it were to be inadvertently left in the open when I have to rushed off due to this emergency."

"OK, OK, fine but this has to be the last time, I will not do it again. The Hammerites would have my head regardless if I abandoned my post again," Johnny replied reluctantly.

With that settled, and feeling both somewhat amazed and slightly guilty for what she had just done, Antheria dashed off down the corridor. She followed the pipes left and right, then left again, up a rusty flight of metal stairs through a sliding door, knowing that following the pipelines was the best way to find your way around the labyrinth of the under city steam tunnels. Taking another left she reached a ladder and climbed up into the colony proper.

She emerged in a large chamber about 2000ft square. Bright blue lights hung down from the ceiling high above her, casting an ultra-violet blue hue throughout the chamber. Antheria was surrounded by many plants and vegetables that provided food for the colony. These plants were kept alive both by the lights powered by the geothermal generator and sprinklers fed by an underground river. Antheria liked this chamber, this was how she imagined the outside world would look like. If she squinted the lights blurred into one, giving it the appearance of a midday blue sky.

Surface

All the lights and sprinklers were powered by geothermal power as was everything else. It was monitoring this power that fell to Antheria, yet she was abandoning this duty at least for now. She knew Luke had already abandoned it before her, well no, abandoning is the wrong word, he was forced to leave. If it can survive without him, it can survive without me, she thought.

She followed the main path in the dirt to the end of the chamber and travelled up some raised metal steps, which led through to a short corridor that emerged in a far larger chamber.

Known simply as Main Shaft, this was the largest open area of the entire underground settlement, Rock could just be seen high above in the dark gloom. Slightly lower and all around shun the distant lights of the various buildings. It was how she imagined the night sky would look like.

Most of the buildings were built out from the rock face itself. Where the rock alone was not enough to support the buildings, additional support was in place including large pillars and where the building was higher up, it was suspended by thick wires and pylons bolted to the ceiling. Each building was interconnected by walkways that were suspended between them.

Quickly Antheria made her way over to the first of the walkways that led towards the centremost building. This

Chapter 1: The Last Ride

building was not built out of the rock, instead it rested on the floor of the chamber and was constructed from the ground up. The shape of the building was that of a hammer. The first several floors made the head of the hammer, and above that, hundreds more floors made the handle. The handle soared upwards and out of sight. Antheria knew that the handle was more than just living and office space for the Hammerites. It also had a far more sinister purpose. For it was within the handle part of the structure that those sentenced to death were to ride the elevator to the surface, never to be seen again, lost to the frozen wasteland above. This was a fate she knew extremely soon would be shared by Luke.

She had to stop this, she must, but how? She found nothing of use in the book that she had so carefully studied, if only there was more time. The charge was ridiculous, betraying the colony, how had he done that? All he did was to trespass. What could be so terrible about visiting the upper levels? She began dashing along the walkway. This was a complete travesty of justice; it was about time that someone made a stand over this, not just for Luke but for all the others before him and those that were to follow.

Antheria burst through the main doors that led through into the courtroom. Maybe she could somehow get him leniency. She was ready to shout her protests, however all her preparations were pointless as she was presented with

Surface

an empty courtroom "Am I too late?", She thought to herself. Quickly and more quietly she headed out of the courtroom to the centre of the building that contained that elevator, the last ride as it was known by some. She stopped short of the elevator as people were gathered there. Quickly she stepped to one side to hide behind some crates. She peeked around the side; she could see three men getting into the lift. She caught sight of one of them, it was Luke. Antheria left her hiding place, but before Luke even had a chance to see her, the doors had closed, and the elevator began to rise.

Now clear of people she ran to the elevator where finally her feelings for him asserted themselves more strongly than ever before, and she could no longer pretend to herself that she was doing this just because of the injustice. She knew now it was because of her feelings for Luke. A tear slowly ran down her cheek as she stood there slightly breathless in front of the sombre military grey doors of the elevator. No longer could she act on these feelings as all hope for love to blossom faded away with the now faint shouts of protests from Luke. Luke's voice like her hopes petered out to nothing.

Chapter 2: The Two Strangers

"How can this be?", Luke thought to himself, his eyes having adjusted to the light. Ahead of Luke was not the frozen wasteland that he was expecting but instead lush green grasslands almost as far as the eye could see with the only exception being the shadows of mountains in the far distance. Where was the ice? The snow and the howling winds? No, there was sunshine. In-fact it was warmer outside than it was back underground.

Luke just could not believe it, from utter fear and dread to near exhilaration in a few seconds. It was out of the frying pan into the lovely warm bath! Before Luke could ask the guards what was going on, and ask them why they and their superiors have been lying to him all these years, Luke was forcefully dragged away from the door and pushed up against an old ruined wall that bordered the grassy meadow in which they were now standing.

The contents of his pockets were quickly emptied before the two Hammerites turned and walked quickly back into the bunker not saying a word. The large metal bunker doors closed behind them with a large clunk. At that moment, Luke realised that this was the end of a life he once knew and of everyone he knew. He knew that he would never see any of the people he once knew again.

Surface

"What… what about Antheria?" he thought to himself. He would also never see her again. If only he had worked up the courage to speak to her, to let her know he wanted things to be closer between them.

Luke was not left to dwell on his own thoughts for long as two strangers began to approach from below, down the hill. Luke strained his eyes in the bright sunlight to try and make out the figures, but all he could make out was the outlines of the figures that now approached. Luke knew nothing about the people on the surface; there should not even be anyone here at all. It was supposed to be a frozen wasteland where no one could survive but this was obviously not true. Luke then wondered if everything that he had been told was also a lie. What about all the other so-called executions, maybe they too were alive up here. or had the ice just now receded? Luke found himself with many questions swirling around in his head. This left him feeling excited that he might meet these people, but also apprehensive, as after all he knew nothing about them and their fate.

Slowly the figures drew closer; he could now make out the features of a woman and a child. The woman was blonde with slightly messy long hair that reached down to her shoulders. Her clothes were like nothing Luke had ever seen, She was wearing a bright green cloak over what looked like leather fashioned armour, the likes of which Luke had read about in history books. The girl who was

Chapter 2: The Two Strangers

holding onto the woman's hand looked to be no more than ten years of age. She had a much darker colour of hair than the woman. Her hair appeared to be tied back in a knot, but before Luke could get a proper look at the child she slid out of view behind the woman. At that moment the woman reached into a pocket on her left and removed something long. Fearing it could be a weapon, Luke edged backwards towards the metal doors of the bunker as she approached ever closer. The woman spoke something, but Luke did not hear. She was now only ten paces away. Luke could not back up any further, the cold metal doors behind him blocked his path.

The woman was now close enough for Luke to make out what she had taken from her pocket was not a weapon, it was just a long narrow loaf of bread, which the woman was now presenting to Luke in an offering gesture. Nerves now calming, and not wanting to offend the woman, Luke stepped forward to reach for the bread. Luke did not say anything as he assumed this stranger from another world would not speak his language.

Luke was about to tuck into the bread when he remembered the child; perhaps he should offer her a piece? Luke realised that he had last sight of the child. She still must be cowering behind this woman, who Luke guessed was probably her mother.

Surface

Luke moved round the woman to reach the child, the woman's eyes followed Luke as he did so. A puzzled expression appeared on her face. Luke pointed to the bread then to his mouth, before pointing to the girl behind the woman. With this gesture the woman just looked even more puzzled; perhaps Luke was not as good a communicator with people as he thought? As he drew around, he was stopped dead in his tracks, not by anything physical, but by a shock. This shock was strangely larger than anything he had experienced throughout this terrible day, even worse than the thought of being put to death only to find out it was life, life forever as an outcast. Yes, this shock was far greater, for the child who Luke had seen just moments ago vanished altogether right in front of him.

Frantically Luke scanned the almost featureless grasslands that surrounded him. There was nowhere she could have gone, surely she could not just have vanished? Perhaps he imagined her?

In the corner of his eye, the same child re-appeared twenty feet to the right, against the stone wall. The child's mouth was open and moving, but no words came out. The child then began to approach him, but she was not walking, she was gliding. Her heels gently brushed the top of grass blades as she levitated over them. Just a few paces from Luke she vanished yet again.

Chapter 2: The Two Strangers

What sounded like a band's drum roll started up in Luke's head. He was beginning to panic now. Was this all a dream? How could this even happen? Stricken with panic and fear of the unknown, Luke's vision began to blur and little fairy lights danced around in his head. Luke's breathing became shallow and faster until he was panting, like a dog on a hot day. Luke barely noticed that the woman was now slowly backing away from him, he could not keep focus any longer.

Darkness began to envelop him as his vision began to get narrower and narrower, as if being constricted by a giant python. The sky became ground, ground became sky and then there was nothing but blackness.

Chapter 3: The Way Out

Rumours were starting to spread throughout the colony about just why Luke was banished, for death to claim him. Some were saying it was because he stumbled upon something he should not have, while others said he had just simply ran foul of some obscure law. In any case, Antheria had to know why. Why also do the authorities decide it should be death for anyone who ventured up into the upper levels? What possibly could be hidden up there? It was for that crime, Antheria believed, Luke was banished for. She had to see for herself, she knew Luke had made it up there plenty of times before without being caught, at least until now. There were many ways to reach the upper levels, however most had become impassable either due to them being blocked off by the authorities, or they had simply collapsed and caved in.

She had heard rumours, however, of one particular route. a route that the Hammerites probably did not know about. a route that even Luke had not dared to venture into.

She decided she would have to take the risk. She packed a few supplies and a torch before setting off and left her small room in the large residential block in the main chamber. She had many hours before her next shift was due to start. So she had plenty of time to look around. She

Chapter 3: The Way Out

reached and climbed the stairs perched against the rock face in a darkened corner of the chamber. Other than a disused building there was nothing else up there. The only exception was one lonely walkway that crossed a fifty foot gap between the building and the rock face.

She followed the walkway, which creaked unnervingly at every step. It was suspended by a few thin steel cables, making her feel like a spider that was hiding in the eaves of an old building. The drop down from the walkway was far, the walkway itself was dusty from under use. Strangely, the walkway went nowhere, it ended at a sheer rock face. At least that was how it looked to the untrained eye, Antheria knew different. Luke had told her that on one of his little adventures he noticed the walkway did in fact go somewhere. There was a hidden entrance slot ten feet up the rock face, above the end of the walkway. Luke never ventured in, but he did once climb part way up, where he noticed a strong breeze emanating from the slot. Rusty bolts in the wall indicated that there was once a staircase going up there, but it had either fallen down or had been removed.

Antheria reached the end of the walkway and glanced at the dizzying distance of the drop below. She swallowed her fear and began to climb the rock face. She quickly found herself in a precarious position where a rock jutting out from the wall blocked her climb and the only way to get around was to shimmy around this obstruction away

Surface

from the safety of the walkway below.

Slowly and nervously she edged her way around the rock pinnacle. As she did so, she knocked off some small stones with her feet. Antheria could not help but track the stones progress as they bounced off the rock face once, then twice before shattering themselves in pieces on the floor below. Antheria began to feel nauseous, her breath quickened.

This was probably where Luke had turned back. Any more stones could alert the authorities, and of course there was the very real possibility she could fall to her death. Her grip began to loosen, she needed to move. With one heavy heave and a whole lot of determination, she grabbed onto a nearby ledge around the pinnacle and swung her small frame around it. In doing so, she caused several more stones and dirt to fall and clatter loudly below.

The sound of clattering was replaced by shouting; someone had spotted her, a Hammerite. "No!" she shouted in her head, "I am not going to let what happened to Luke happen to me too". With strength like that shown by a mother lifting a fallen boulder off of her trapped child, she hauled herself up into the tiny opening before landing inside where she sprawled out on the floor, panting.

Antheria moved quickly into the passage and did not stop until she was far clear of the drop and the people chasing

Chapter 3: The Way Out

her. Shouts could be still be heard and were now growing nearer. Boots on metal started to echo around the small, dank passage in which she now stood. Antheria set off again deep into the darkness. She made progress along the tight passage that grew darker as she went. She reached for her maintenance torch and switched it on. Eerie shadows were cast on the walls as the light shone through the various old decaying wooden beams that held up the roof. She shined the torch down the passage to reveal a lattice of beams arranged like match sticks holding up the roof from various angles as the floor and ceiling began to slope upwards.

Antheria progressed along the passage where she tripped several times over the beams. The passage continued to get steeper until it was near vertical. She was now using the wooden and metal beams like a giant climbing frame. With the torch in her mouth, she progressed up the precarious shaft. She noticed that she could not hear the others, but they were most likely still in pursuit. Higher still she climbed, the shaft changing character. The beams of the shaft where replaced by stone, and old metal ladders allowed her to make upwards progress. All the time Antheria was scared, one false move could spell her doom. Finally, a short horizontal section provided a welcome respite before another shaft continued upwards out of sight. She knew now that she was likely heading to the surface, she would press on until it came too cold,

Surface

hopefully the Hammerites would not follow this far.

As she climbed this shaft, she began to become aware of a dim light that was not of her own. Shortly there was a soft breeze that quickly grew into a howling gale. This wind was refreshing, yet it was not a cold wind. As she got closer and closer, she was stopped by large boulders that were jammed across the shaft. These boulders were precariously wedged together to form an uneasy rock ceiling. However, there was a way through, Antheria followed the now bright light as she uneasily squirmed her way through.

She emerged, at first she could not see anything blinded by the natural light. Soon her vision adjusted, and she gazed upwards to be greeted by the silvery white clouds of a damp afternoon. She climbed out of the hole and onto fertile grasslands that stretched out below her, which sloped gently down to a large forest in the distance.

This was all she imagined the surface would have been like from all the books she had read and screens she had seen. Except where was the ice? She collapsed to her knees. "So this was the truth? Was everyone being kept prisoner under false pretences believing the world above was an icy wasteland? Perhaps this was a ploy to make sure that the people had no choice except to support the colony, trapped down there like rats? That must be why they got rid of Luke fearing that he might be too close to

Chapter 3: The Way Out

finding out the truth? Perhaps he had once made it to the surface, but if that was the case why had he protested so much knowing what was up here?

She was angry, she felt like charging straight back in down the hole to confront them. The thought that maybe Luke and the others were not dead drove her to continue through this strange new land. A noise could be heard from down the hole. Had the Hammerites followed her?

Chapter 4: The Red Way

Slowly Luke opened his eyes as one by one his senses began to awake. His eyes could see that he was in a small room with stone walls and that he was lying on a straw bed. His hearing awoke next, he heard the pitter patter of rain drops falling on the roof above him. Next his sense of smell awoke, detecting the smell of cooking meat. Finally, it was the sense of touch and pain as a dull throbbing began to assert itself in his shoulder.

Luke studied his surroundings carefully. To the left of him sat on an unvarnished wooden stool, on top of which was a metal bowl with faint steamy vapour emanating from it. Someone must have been caring for him while he was unconscious, but who and why?

Luke slowly and cautiously slid out of bed and rose to his unsteady feet. A sudden bout of dizziness almost sent him straight back down again as he staggered towards the wooden door that led out of the room.

He could hear the rain louder now, he felt a cold draft brush against his skin as he reached for the handle of the door. The draft made him realise that he was not wearing anything but an undergarment. Beyond the door, he could clearly hear the footsteps of at least two people

Chapter 4: The Red Way

approaching, so in his half naked, half-awake state Luke quickly jumped back into the bed and closed his eyes before the approaching people could see that he was awake.

The two people burst into the room arguing and at first Luke could not understand what they were saying for their heavy accents cloaked the fact they were in-fact speaking his language. "Regardless, we should not have brought him here," a male voice proclaimed.

"What else could we have done? Leave him on the road? He could have been eaten by scavengers, or worse, taken off by the bandits," a woman replied.

Luke opened one eye. The man was hidden from view by the pillow, but he could see the woman, she was the one he had met outside the bunker.

"He is not our problem, you know the Elders policy on newcomers, Ellana. You should never have persuaded me to help you bring him here." Then the man sighed, "Look as soon as he has recovered enough, get him out of here before the village elders find out about him."

The man stomped out of the room and violently closed the door behind him. Luke thought this would be a good time to reveal to her that he was in-fact conscious.

Surface

Ellana spoke to Luke in a much softer voice than she had just been using just moments before, "So, you are awake? You have been dead to the world for almost all of the daylight hours".

"So… you dragged me here?," Luke questioned.

"Yes," Ellana replied simply before adding, "You were lucky that Regarus was near by and could be persuaded to help me, though he argued against me all the way."

"Why?," Luke paused and then spoke the simple words, "Thank you".

She seemed to ignore the praise; perhaps it was the words from Regarus ringing in her ears. "As soon as you are feeling better, you must leave," she said in reply.

"Why?" Luke questioned, "Is it the Elders?" Luke wished he had not said that as he remembered he was pretending to be asleep when that was said.

"So you were awake then? As you no doubt heard, outsiders are not welcome here. Trouble always seems to follow you outsiders."

"Trouble?," Luke questioned

"Yes, trouble. Trouble that others would not allow to come

Chapter 4: The Red Way

to pass." Curtly Ellana added, "Well, you are fit enough to leave now. Here, I will fetch you some food and water, then you must go, tonight. Make sure no one sees you, I am not sure what they would do to you or me for that matter."

Before Luke could reply Ellana left the room and closed the door. Five minutes or so later she returned with a bowl of some sort of steaming hot beef stew. "Here take this, you will need it". As she handed Luke the stew Luke noticed a peculiar scar on the back of her hand; it was shaped like an eight-pronged star. Noticing Luke's gaze Ellana quickly withdrew her hand.

"Tonight, take the path out of the village up the valley. Follow the path until you reach a waterfall. Behind this you will find a passage. Follow the passage until you emerge near the main road. Once there take the right fork and follow the road downhill until you reach Brinns Reach," she said.

"Brinns reach?", Luke asked.

"Yes, Brinns Reach, that is where you came from, is it not? Well if it isn't, I am sure you can find your way from there," Ellana said.

Silence fell, giving Luke time to think. The more he thought about this journey to the strange town, the more

Surface

Luke grew concerned for his own safety. He did not fancy an encounter with these Bandits or Scavengers. Luke had to ask for more help from Ellana, despite the help she had already rendered in dragging him to safety.

"I've overheard you talking about the dangers out there, surely I would not get far out there alone and unarmed". Ellana thought for a moment before speaking, "Well, I guess I can take you as far as the road, but from there on you are on your own. Whatever you do though, stay on the road, it is well lit and so should be clear of scavengers."

"Scavengers? Yes, what are they?", Luke asked.

"You have not heard of them? I thought they were almost everywhere. They're ghastly creatures, not generally aggressive on their own, unless they sense a weakness. Be warned, however. they are truly ruthless creatures in a pack, even the light of the brightest fire does not keep them away when a group of them smells fresh meat. They would settle for carrion, but fresh meat is far tastier and trust me, you and me are as fresh as they come".

Within hours, Luke found himself standing outside the stone house looking out into the darkness. He was dressed in his old clothes but, thankfully, he had been provided with a warm green cloak to keep the cold night air away. The design of the cloak was remarkably similar to the one Ellana had been wearing. He carried a torch, too, that

Chapter 4: The Red Way

burnt hot tar, the remnants of which slowly dripped down the handle towards Luke's unprotected hands.

The village around him was only small; there could not have been more than eight buildings. Most of the buildings were simple stone structures, however, one did stand out from the rest. This was a much larger building than the others, it sat on the other side of the valley, perching on top a small hill, making it tower over the village even more. The only access seemed to be by a small stone bridge that stretched over a black void that separated the building from the village.

The building had two large well-lit stained glass windows that were glowing ominously, giving it the appearance of an ever present eagle waiting for is prey.

Luke scanned the rest of his surroundings, and his gaze was soon drawn away from the building to the high cliffs that he could see surrounding the village. As his eyes grew accustomed to the darkness, he could see that the whole village was at the bottom of vast gash in the earth. Only a small patch of the starry sky could be seen above. The overhanging cliffs obscured the rest.

"Come on, there is no time to wait, quickly before we are seen." Ellana said. Hurriedly she pushed him onwards along the path that led away from the village. The path began to narrow now, towering cliffs on the left, and to

Surface

the right the ground dropped away into the darkness, where a distant stream could be heard. As they continued along, the sound of the stream below grew louder until it became a roar. At this point, the path began to ascend steeply on the left; Ellana did not slow her pace if anything she moved even faster.

As they ascended the source of the roar became visible to them in the torchlight. In front of them was an enormous waterfall some fifty feet high and as wide as several houses. The roar was now deafening. Water began to splash their faces and dampen the torches. The path continued into the waterfall where it appeared to vanish. Following the path they could see that in fact the path went around the waterfall to the left. With only one torch going out, they made it behind the waterfall, where a small tunnel could be seen. The tunnel climbed steeply for a short while before stopping at a blank wall with a wooden ladder. Ellana climbed first before shouting to Luke to come up. He climbed, passing several platforms before the shaft narrowed to just over body sized. A hefty breeze brushed Luke's cheeks as Ellana pushed open a wooden hinged lid at the top. They emerged above the waterfall on the other side of the bank.

A short scramble through an overgrown path brought them onto a stone paved road. This road was well lit by torches. It could be seen meandering down the hillside in front of them like a two-headed snake as the road forked

Chapter 4: The Red Way

just in front of them. "This is where I must leave you, just follow the right hand road and do not stray, keep a look out for scavengers and good luck", Ellana said with a wave of her hand.

"Thank you for what you have done", said Luke. With that Ellana left him to the eerie glow of the torches on the road.

Now alone and the sound of the water distant, Luke was more aware of the strange noises that surrounded him. Chirps and squeaks of various creatures could be heard, as well as cracking and snapping of the undergrowth. Luke's heart rate began to quicken with every new sound. His own heart added its own instrument to the symphony of sounds around him. But one noise stood out among the rest, the sound of footsteps, at least it sounded like footsteps. They were coming from behind him. He quickly looked around. As he did so there was a rustle of something slipping into the undergrowth, but there was nothing to be seen. Someone or something was following him. The path continued to sweep downwards below him as it snaked its way down into a valley. Luke started to quicken his pace, the steps behind quickened too. Luke broke into a run and then a sprint down hill.

There must have been a loose paving stone or something similar for the next thing Luke knew he was going head over heels straight off the path through bushes and undergrowth that scratched at his face and limbs as he

Surface

tumbled past. His tumbling changed to a fall as he fell backwards over a cliff. He came to a bone crunching halt on a leaf strewn muddy ground a short distance below. Luke grabbed for the torch that now lay at his side; adrenaline blocking any pain he had been feeling. As he grabbed for the torch, he could hear twittering and cracking in the bushes above him.

"Thud". Then a louder "Thud!". Then "CRASH!". A creature some four-foot tall emerged near by, It's clear wings could be seen glittering off the torchlight. The wings looked far too small to lift its heavy grasshopper like bulk, and it was at least twenty paces away. Luke only needed to get up and flee. The wings did, however, appear to allow the creature to jump large distances as it fluttered is wings, compressed its back legs and immediately cleared the gap between it and Luke. This was before Luke had even managed to get to his feet. The creature now bore down on him; its sharp brown mandibles sought his flesh.

Luke swung his torch at the creature, causing it to flinch and take another great leap away from him, before rebounding off the cliff face and crashing down onto him. Luke instinctively raised the torch above his head, using both arms, just in time to stop the creatures sharpened mandibles piercing his flesh. The creature pushed its weight down on him as he lay there on the ground. Luke was now almost strangling himself with his own torch as it was pushed against his neck. All the time the creature's

Chapter 4: The Red Way

mandibles were stabbing at him trying to reach his face.

Luke kicked up with his legs, striking the creature's soft underbelly; this only stopped it for a second. The creature jumped back, once again against the cliff wall, before crashing back into Luke. The, ferocity of this attack knocked the air from Luke's lungs and caused the torch to fly from his hands. Again the creature bore down on him. Luke covered his head in a futile attempt to protect himself from the coming fatal blow. But it never came; instead he heard a loud squeal. Luke slowly uncovered his eyes to see a figure plunging a sword deep into the creature's underbelly as it now laid helplessly upside down. Yellow fluids sprayed them both as the creature made one last loud squeal before becoming rigid and then collapsing into a lifeless heap.

"Well that was a spot of bother you got yourself into," the man said.

"Thank you, yet again I have been saved by a stranger. Who are you?", Luke said, with a highly relieved face.

"Aaron Spudtaker is me name" he said, "Come on hop hop, get it hop hop… never mind, let's get back on the road before more of these creatures turn up to the party."

Aaron was not a particularly tall chap, standing slightly smaller than Luke, though he looked far more robust and

Surface

well built than Luke. He was dressed in leathers of intensely dark colours. His jacket and trousers were adorned with many pockets and pouches. On his back, Luke could just see the arm and string of what looked like some kind of bow; the majority of which was hidden from view by Aaron's dark brown cloak.

Aaron sheathed his sword under his leather jacket before stooping over to pick up Luke's torch. He then offered Luke his hand and helped him to his feet. Standing next to Aaron, Luke could now see Aaron's facial features more clearly, at least he would have been able to if the features in question were not obscured by several weeks of unkempt hair. Still, the hair gave Aaron the rugged appearance that most women would hanker for and most men know not to mess with. There was one point on Aaron's face that was not obscured by hair, it lay on his chin where an old scar prevented growth.

Aaron guided Luke back up the steep hill next to the small cliff Luke had just tumbled down earlier, and within a few moments Luke and Aaron were back on the road. As they began walking the adrenaline pumping around Luke's body started to subside. Luke now felt his every bruise; his whole body ached painfully, the worst pain being that of his shoulder, already injured by his blackout earlier.

A few minutes of silence passed as they trudged down the road, Aaron decided to break the silence. "So, what were

Chapter 4: The Red Way

you doing off the road in the dark? Is being eaten by scavengers a hobby of yours?"

"One of them was tracking me, I ran to get away I simply tripped and landed where you found me." Luke replied defensively, His pride was slightly hurt now as well. "Speaking of which, just how is it you came to be here anyway?" Luke enquired. "Don't get me wrong, I am not ungrateful that you were there," Luke said.

"Well…" Aaron paused, "you see…" Aaron paused again, "I heard an affray just off the road and thought I would go and investigate, see if I could help, you know because I am such a chivalrous person." "Good thing I did too," he added.

"Then how is it that I did not see you on the road then?," Luke asked immediately, wishing he had not.

"Fine… did not think you would believe that. OK. Yes, I was following you, I thought you would have a few coin". Luke suddenly stopped walking and stared at Aaron not taking his eyes off of him.

"You were going to rob me?," Luke said with a shocked expression on his face.

"Yep," Aaron replied simply. "But I see now that you have nothing of value at all otherwise you would have had

Surface

more than a torch to defend yourself with."

Sensing Luke's distinct dislike of the act he would have performed, Aaron went on to say "Listen, it's not like I do this because I want to, I do it because I have to. You know how hard it is to earn a decent living without being born into it." Luke did not reply.

"Well let me tell you then, it's as hard as climbing a cliff with your teeth. Well at least it feels like it."

"Well just do not try anything," Luke said, although feeling slightly placated. Luke now did not want to pursue the subject as Aaron did not seem to pose him any immediate harm, and after all, he had just saved him from becoming bug food.

"So…" Aaron began.

"So?," Luke replied.

"Let's not beat around the bush, I can see you're an outsider, I mean who wears clothes like that? I mean white and green, that is just asking for trouble if you ask me. Let me guess, you are from the under colony?"

Luke nodded in response.

"I am an outsider too of sorts, as in I am not welcome in

Chapter 4: The Red Way

most places for one reason or another." Aaron paused and mulled over what he would say next.

"Well, tell you what err… what is your name?"

"Luke"

"Well, tell you what Luke, as you are a fellow outsider in a way and we seem to be getting on oh so well together, how do you fancy being my partner in crime as it were and team up for a bit? Hey you might even be useful." Aaron almost sniggered slightly at his last remark.

"Useful?," Luke asked.

"Yeah, if the guards are coming after me I can just throw you in their way to make a getaway," Aaron laughed, Luke was not amused, "You don't laugh much do you, Luke?"

Luke replied, "With the day I have been having, no I don't".

"The day you have been having?," Aaron repeated in a slightly annoyed tone.

"Let me tell you about my day, I have just escaped out of the town jail where I was put for something I did not actually do for once. I lost all my loo... err possessions in the process. Then on the road I was chased by bandits, a

Surface

lot less respectable than me, I can tell you. Oh, and to top it all I had to rescue this badly dressed outsider from a hungry Scavenger. So don't talk to me about bad days".

Luke did not respond.

The two walked in silence for a period down the winding torch lit road; the welcoming lights of Brinns Reach could now be seen on the horizon. Aaron was the one who broke the silence again.

"So how about it? Partners? Us outsiders should stick together. It is better odds".

Luke thought about it for a while. Of course, joining up with Aaron did not seem like a particularly sane thing to do, but on the other-hand Luke had very few supplies, as well as no currency, presuming they even used currency. He basically knew nothing about this world. Luke realised he had no choice if he wanted to survive.

Reluctantly, Luke shook Aaron's hand and the deal was made.

"Excellent, though it's got to be a seventy, thirty split for someone with so little experience as yourself," Aaron said.

Then out of nowhere Aaron brought up another topic, "So have you heard about 'em children sightings then?"

Chapter 5: Child Games

Luke and Aaron stopped at an inn just before entering the settlement proper. The place looked quite decrepit. The inside and the innkeeper did not look much better. The innkeeper and Aaron had a brief chat outside of Luke's earshot, making Luke marginally suspicious, especially as the innkeeper never seemed to take his eye off him, despite talking to Aaron. Aaron slipped the innkeeper a couple pieces of rectangular metal. The innkeeper grunted, before nodding his head, to a shed around the back of the inn.

The shed was barely that. The floor was mainly grassed over; there was no roof except in one corner to protect the hay stacked there from getting wet. Aaron collected, or more likely stole firewood and piled it in another corner away from the hay. He then lit the fire using a flint and a piece of metal that were concealed in one of his many jacket pockets.

To most a shed without a roof would be an exceptionally poor place to spend the night, however, to Luke it was heaven. He was awe-inspired as he gazed up at the stars in all their glory. He still had not gotten used to this new sky, it was nothing like he imagined from what he had read. This caused goose bumps to shoot up and down Luke's body.

Surface

They set about bedding down for the night. Luke borrowed some hay and Aaron used a rolled up blanket from his backpack. It was not as cold as Luke would have thought, the old brick walls of the shed were doing a good job of reflecting the heat of the fire back on them. The roar of the flames drowned out the drunken laughter and sound of broken glass from the tavern. Shortly Luke's world drifted away.

Aaron stayed up a while longer, even getting himself an ale or two from the inn when it quietened down. He eventually placed the last few of the collected logs onto the fire and drifted off to sleep.

Aaron "awoke", not to a ruined shed and smouldering embers of a fire, but instead to far more grandeur surroundings. There in his new surroundings, his mouth was ajar, for he was sat in a hall of what seemed like a palace. The floor was paved with grey marble, lined with gold intricate designs that almost seemed to dance in their complexity. These depicted many strange symbols and patterns. The hall contained little furniture, save for the throne that he was sat on. The throne itself was covered in the finest purple silks that felt both smooth and soft to the touch.

"Now this is more like it," Aaron thought to himself.

Chapter 5: Child Games

Aaron knew it was a dream, but at the same time he was happy to pretend it was not. Two large doors at the opposite end of the hall flung open. Aaron expected to see a king or queen, but instead it was a small girl that now approached from the opening. She had brown hair and looked to be around nine or ten years old, with a crystal clear complexion. She stopped only a few paces from his throne.

"I see my lord is enjoying his splendour," she said.

"Indeed I am. Pray tell, why did I dream you up? At least why did I not dream you up, ten years older?"

The girl giggled. "Silly man, you have not dreamt me. I am here as a messenger. All this here is real, at least it will be if you do what is needed of you".

"And that is?," Aaron questioned.

"Well," and after a short pause, "it really is quite simple. Keep the man you travel with alive, and ensure he succeeds, then through him you will gain great riches."

Aaron thought this was still his mind playing tricks in this dream, but he decided to play along for now "How does that make me rich and what mission?" Aaron asked.

The girl gave a quick smile, "His mission I cannot say, but

Surface

what I can tell you is that he will become a powerful man, a man of influence in certain societies. I have heard that with enormous power comes enormous wealth". Aaron knew at least that last statement was true. Power, influenced in the right way, could bring many riches. Before he could ask more, the girl simply vanished and the dream faded away with the morning's light.

Luke too dreamt that same night. He dreamt that he was in fantastical ice landscape, where massive ice pillars jutted out of the ground as far as the eye could see. In one direction beyond the ice, there was a great pit as wide as a city. Thick black smoke billowed out of the hole, like the smoke of a massive funeral pyre that obscured anything that resided within. Luke could not only see how cold it was here, but he could also feel it. The cold was biting into him like a thousand tiny daggers. This is how he imagined the surface would be like, nothing but a bleak ice desert. In that moment, he wished above all else, to be back home in his warm bed.

He was distracted from the cold at that moment as a child appeared from the direction of the pit. This child looked exactly like the one who haunted him before, outside the bunker. Fear and panic began to set in as before, and the familiar sound of the drum roll began to play in his head. The child opened her mouth, but this time words did come "Be wary," she said in a very non childlike girl's voice, sounding more like several hundred people speaking at

Chapter 5: Child Games

once rather than one girl "Be wary, of the man you travel with, for he will betray!"

Luke responded rather shakily, "Betray, betray who? Me? But why? ... He is a thief, so what? He will steal from me? But I have nothing for him to steal!"

The child answered Luke's many questions with a simple nod of her head before repeating. "He will betray you" in her strange voice.

"How do you know this?," Luke asked, wondering why he should believe her.

The girl ignored the question and continued: "Know this, to travel alone will spell your doom." The child vanished as she did before. His heart rate slowed. The frozen world, in which he stood, once again came to the forefront of his mind; the cold was almost unbearable now.

"Hello? Is anybody there?," he shouted as he shivered.

The white of the ice and snow began to glow brighter and brighter. "Perhaps I am suffering from snow blindness?" he thought.

Eventually everything became a brilliant white; even the smoke was invisible now. Luke was no longer standing, he was falling, falling through infinite white. He could feel

Surface

the wind rushing past his face, and it was getting stronger and louder. Then out of whiteness below came a green blur. Soon it became clearer what this blur was as the whiteness faded to blue skyies above the landscape below. It was lush and green patched with farms and settlements. He could see a path snaking off across the ground and a large solitary building directly below. This building was growing larger as his fall continued. He now recognised the building, it was the inn. He was getting close to the ground now, close enough to see Aaron walking from the shed to the inn. The ground finally rushed up towards him, and he felt a sudden impact.

He awoke; startled, and stood up quickly out of his makeshift bed where he almost knocked himself out on the wooden enclosure that was protecting the hay. He may not have felt pain from the impact in his dream, but he certainly felt that.

After getting his composure back, he looked around to find that Aaron had gone, so he had not imagined him walking off, coincidence he concluded? Luke calmed and began to think. He was not sure what to do now. Why should he trust this child, this strange girl? She already made him black out for almost an entire day previously. On the other hand, why should he trust this stranger, a thief nonetheless?

"Aaron did save me from that beast," Luke thought again.

Chapter 5: Child Games

Luke wandered into the inn to look for Aaron. After a brief look around the rather foul smelling empty bar, Luke spotted him sitting at a table off to the corner. Aaron was already tucking into his breakfast.

"Sorry mate, I was starving this morning, just had to eat," Aaron said as he waved to the tavern owner to come over.

"So..." Luke mused, "Call me blunt if you like, but do you mind telling me more about yourself? I mean since we are going to be sticking together." Luke was eager to know more about Aaron as the dream had made him even more wary about him.

"Not much to say really, I came from a poor family as you might have guessed. We lived in the lowlands to the west, near the coast. We barely scraped a living off the land. I came to the towns looking for wealth and adventure as I was bored of life at home. I found, however that there was none to be had, at least no wealth that is, well any gained by honest means." He paused for a sip of mead and continued, "I learned very quickly it was every man for himself, I took what I needed and never looked back. You do what you have to, to survive in this harsh world." Aaron said in an unusual non-jovial tone. "Here," he said, changing the subject. "Did you have any unusual dreams last night, possibly involving children and riches?" Luke's eyes widened in surprise.

Surface

"So… I am not the only one to see these children?" Luke thought to himself, without responding verbally.

"Well?" Aaron asked rather impatiently.

Luke chose his words carefully. "Yes, but it's not important, is it?"

"Not important?!" Aaron said loudly, "Of course it's blooming important, have you not heard of the tales of the children? I suppose you would not have living where you lived. Well they say that if you were to follow the children and complete the tasks they set, you will be rewarded with treasurers beyond your wildest dreams. And you say that is not important?"

"But it was just a dream" Luke interjected.

"Listen, if you don't want to tell me then fine, but I think you should do whatever the children have told you and of course take me along for the ride. Be warned though there are those who think the children are evil and, therefore those who follow them are evil. But in my view that is a lot of superstitious nonsense, and like all manure like that it should be ignored and avoided with the contempt it deserves. Just keep any mentioning of them between you and me, okay?"

Chapter 5: Child Games

Aaron could see that Luke was still not convinced "If you still do not believe me about the children, then let us head to the monks of the Chalice in the east, they know all about 'em children. Proof of their past deeds," Luke found himself nodding his head in agreement, he had to learn about these children that inhabit this New World, what is it they want from him. He hoped this would not be a fools errand and wondered the real reason why Aaron, a thief, would want to go there. Aaron, as if sensing Luke's question, spoke the obvious.

"Look, while you're getting all pally with those monks, I will be helping myself to their valuables. You will learn about the children and be able to do whatever it is they want of you and I will make some nice chits along the way." Luke was not in the slightest bit shocked at this, he was getting to know what sort of person Aaron was.

"So I am to be the distraction, then?," Luke questioned, Aaron nodded and held out his hand once again.

Luke found his own hand joining Aaron's, they shook on it. What choice did he have? He wanted to know more, but this was yet another deal he immediately regretted. To Luke it felt as if he were being led down a dark track, the destination of which was as murky as the metaphor.

It was obvious that Aaron, despite trying to convince Luke, did not himself believe in the children either, but what

Surface

better excuse was there to go and help himself to the treasures of the Temple of the Chalice. If somehow what the children said was indeed true, then all the better, Aaron thought.

The innkeeper finally made his way lazily to the table where Luke and Aaron were sat. "Breakfast for my mate here," Aaron requested.

The innkeeper ever silent held out his hand. Aaron removed some strange metal pieces of varying size and colours from one of his pockets. These pieces were rectangular in shape, coloured jade, bronze and silver. There was no gold visible. Luke guessed these pieces passed for currency in this land and that these must be what the "chits" Aaron mentioned earlier were. Luke guessed that the various size and types of metal determined the worth of the chit, a lot more primitive when compared to the electronic currently he used to use.

Aaron handed one large and two small jade chits to the innkeeper. The grumpy innkeeper closed his hand, turned around and left. After a short while, he returned with a plate of some kind of "meat stew". This was placed rather unceremoniously down in front of Luke, almost splattering him in giblets. The meat was unidentifiable, but nonetheless it did not smell too foul.

Luke tucked into his breakfast, with every bite he felt more

Chapter 5: Child Games

able to take on whatever the day ahead had to throw at him. The day "threw" something at him almost straight away after a small bone from his stew became lodged in his throat. It was not choking him, but it caused him to cough and splutter until he was able to extract the offending item. Good start, he thought.

"Careful now, the innkeeper don't give any refunds if the food kills you," Aaron sniggered.

Chapter 6: The Thieves Way

"There is one thing I forget to mention about going to see these monks...," Aaron spoke as they meandered their way through a market, passing many stalls that were set up in the main town square. Each stall had a different coloured covering and dressing indicating what it sold, green and brown for vegetables and fruit, Brown and white parchment, bound tomes and maps, Gold and orange for jewellery and so on. These markings made the whole market a fantastical colourful feast for the eye. It looked almost like the very sun had exploded and all the colours from the sun's light had splashed down and painted the stalls of the paved market square. The market was alive with the sound of people and life. People were shouting about their various wares, while others vigorously haggled, most of it in foreign tongues or exceptionally strong accents, making it difficult for Luke to understand any of it.

They approached a brown and white stall that was brimming over with rolled up parchments. Just before reaching the stall Aaron continued what he was saying, "This is only a slight oversight I promise," he slightly sniggered to himself. "Thing is this journey we are about to set out on is not going to be a simple stroll through the hills. There will be more of 'em creatures where we are

Chapter 6: The Thieves Way

going, bandits too. I can tell you they are not all as charismatic as me."

They stopped just short of the stall. Aaron paused; he reached into one of his many pockets and took out a small mirror. He angled it so that it reflected the morning sun onto someone in the crowd. He did this three times before returning it to his pocket. Quickly a red haired street urchin began pushing and swerving his way through the crowd. His sudden appearance in front of Aaron startled Luke, as the ghostly children were still fresh in his mind. This child, however was no apparition. Aaron flicked the child a small Jade chit. The child immediately took a cheeky bow, then went straight to the stall in front of them with only a slight nod of a command from Aaron.

The stall owner was not happy seeing the boy and immediately began shouting at him. The boy was about to give the overweight stall owner something really to be angry about. The boy took a quill from where it rested and set off running. The stall owner was so stunned by this blatant daylight robbery that he just stood there like a frozen statue. He soon came to his senses and quickly set off into the crowd after the thieving urchin, huffing and puffing as he went. Several others noticed what had happened and set off in pursuit, leaving the area around the stall quite vacant.

After watching this spectacle, Luke turned around to ask

Surface

Aaron what was going on, but he was not there. In the confusion, Aaron had crept forwards and positioned himself behind some barrels near the stall. He then took out something that could only be described as an extendable pole and levered one of the parchments from the table and onto the pole. He tapped the bottom of the pole, which caused it to collapse in on itself, bringing the scroll to him.

Aaron turned and crept back to where Luke was standing. He carefully lifted his coat revealing the parchment he had stolen. It was a map, the title of which clearly read "Eastern Foothills, Graisland".

Aaron browsed for a short period, letting everyone calm down before repeating the same trick several more times in different parts of the market. He acquired a dagger in its scabbard for Luke, some warm clothes for them both and quite a few more chits in a coin box with a convenient handle.

Aaron spent some of these new chits at the most mundane looking stalls. These stalls were still colourful, but they were not as pristine as the others were, they also sported no unnecessary luxuries, just the basics. He bought food as well as other amenities for their journey. Luke wondered why he simply did not rob these stalls too until he realised things like cabbage would probably be quite difficult to get on the end of a pole. Luke also noticed that

Chapter 6: The Thieves Way

the stall owners Aaron was purchasing from seemed quite a bit poorer than the others. Instead of wearing fineries such as silk and fur, these stall owners wore tattered leather and more practical clothing that allowed ease of movement in a day spent labouring and haggling.

They had just finished all their business in the market when Aaron passed the map stall he had robbed earlier. As he passed, he suddenly heard the most dreaded word that could be heard in a career such as his. "THIEF!", the stall owner shouted while pointing at Aaron. More precisely he was pointing at the piece of parchment sticking out from inside of Aaron's jacket, where the title "Eastern Foothills" was clearly legible in a large bold typeface. Before Luke could react, Aaron had already gone. Several stall owners as well as several more armed guards sprinted off in pursuit of him, followed up at the rear by the map stall owner wheezing all the way.

Although Luke did not trust Aaron fully, he thought he at least owed him for the rescue yesterday. That and he needed him to get to the Temple. Luke had to think on his feet, so he started to run in a slightly different direction than Aaron. He then shouted, "Thief! I see the thief!". To his surprise several of the men broke off from the main group and headed in the direction Luke was going. They overtook Luke as they ran down a narrow alley in pursuit of an invisible assailant.

Surface

Luke continued to run until the others were out of view. His shoulder throbbed painfully from his previous day's adventure. He slowed to a walk and was now alone in a dingy sandstone paved alley. The alley was remarkably quiet, a complete contrast to the market. The shouts of the guards and the merchants peddling their goods had gone only to be replaced by the buzzing of flies and the occasional scurry of rodents in the street guttering.

Luke paused for a short while wondering what to do next, before deciding the best thing he could do was to head back to the inn and hope that Aaron would think to meet him there. Luke began walking slowly back the way he came, and as he did so, he passed through the long shadows of the morning sun. He noticed many shapes lurking in the shadows but could not make them out clearly until he entered the shadows himself. Some of the shapes were simply pots and barrels, others were not. A hand reached out from one of the shadows. Luke jumped in surprise at the sudden appearance of it.

"Spare some chits?," the owner of the hand said.

Luke shakily said, "No… all out, sorry". The beggar in the shadow groaned in response. Luke gestured apologetically before continuing to walk the way he had come. He soon reached a crossroad where he paused, making sure the way ahead was the way he had come from.

Chapter 6: The Thieves Way

"Pssst". Luke ignored it, thinking it to be another beggar or worse. "Pssst" again, this time louder. Luke continued to ignore it. A grape hit Luke right on the back of his head. Luke turned around to confront whoever had thrown it.

"Winter's breath," the voice said. "If you do not respond to a simple 'Pssst', then I don't think much of our new partnership." It was Aaron, of course, hunkered down on a flat roof of one of the many low-rise buildings that surrounded the alley. Luke for some reason found the remark quite funny and could not stop himself from bursting out in laughter. Aaron joined in before quickly shushing himself and Luke in case anyone was still around looking for him.

Aaron led the way in the opposite direction to the way Luke was heading, all the time being careful to stay off the main streets. Quickly they wove their way through the alleyways until eventually they reached the outside wall of the town. It appeared as if the wall was not designed for defensive purposes it was probably there just to mark the boundary of the town. As such, the wall only stood just under eight feet high. Aaron gave Luke a quick leg up, before nimbly climbing over it himself. Both safely down on the other side, they quickly put some distance between themselves and the angry mob in the town and started the long trek east.

Perhaps if they had known they were going to be chased

Surface

out of town by an angry mob they could have bought or more likely stolen a horse, but there was no way they could get back into that town now. The townspeople also would have probably realised by now that Luke was Aaron's accomplice, so he could go in alone either. No, they would have to trek on foot.

Several hours passed on the hike, the sun was now high in the sky and the heat of the day was in full swing. They stopped at a traveller's spring at the side of the road and filled their canteens with water. Luke admired the scenery. They were standing in a shallow valley, covered in thick grasses and wild flowers. A light breeze lazily wafted the grass, creating waves of colours that travelled down the valley. Various scents of wild flowers filled the air, summer it seemed was in full swing.

Beyond, further down the valley, Luke could see the hollowed out shells of old farmhouses that had long ago fallen in to disrepair and ruin. Even further in the distance, the ghostly outlines of tall mountains could barely be seen. Luke was not sure if they were indeed mountains or just low clouds on the far horizon.

While Luke was admiring this, Aaron kept his eyes fixed on the ruins, suspicious of what might lay in wait.

With their canteens now filled to the brim, they set off further down the road, making sure to skirt the old ruins.

Chapter 6: The Thieves Way

Several more hours went by as they followed the road, the sun was getting low to the horizon, the land grew cooler. Aaron without warning veered straight off the unevenly paved road. Luke dutifully followed, and they both began to climb steadily up the gentle slopes of the valley's side. Reaching the top they came across an old goat track which they then followed down into the next.

"We have to stay off the main road now" Aaron said, "We are getting close to bandit territory. Going this way means that we may be have to deal with 'em creatures instead, but that would be far better than being force fed our own what-it's by 'em bandits."

They continued along the goat track, there was not a soul to be seen anywhere. But every so often they would hear a rustle of grass, or a strange clicking sound coming from thick undergrowth that now surrounded the path. Probably more creatures, Luke suspected, but so far the creatures appeared to stay clear.

Just in time, with dusk drawing ever closer, Aaron found a handy bare bit of ground on which to make camp, not wanting to risk a night trek with those creatures about. Sheer weight and bulk prevented them from carrying full fabric tents, but instead, animal skins provided fine substitute coverings. They used a line of string and stretched it between two trees before adding the skins to make an adequate shelter. Once the shelter had been set

Surface

up Luke and Aaron gathered wood from a nearby thicket to make a campfire. They lit the fire and heartedly ate a meal of vegetables and a wild rabbit that had strayed too close to the camp. After the meal, they both fell into a restful sleep with their stomachs full and their legs weary. They had no dreams that night.

They awoke in the morning to the dawn chorus. There was evidence of creature activity, such as strange footprints that seemed to have circled the camp, but none of them had seemed to venture close. Aaron had made sure to leave no food out in the open and had provided the fire with enough wood so that it would burn most of the night.

They travelled for several more days, where the terrain gradually changed from lazy grassy hills to forests, before becoming a steeper and rougher terrain. High hills now bordered the small trail they walked, the once distant mountains could now be seen clearly, looming over them, high on the horizon. The soil was thinner here, and white limestone rocks jutted out from the ground all around them.

While travelling, every so often they would catch the glimpse of something in the corner of their eyes, only for nothing to be there when they turned around "Trick of the light," Luke said to himself. The noises were still occurring too, twigs cracked when they passed through woods and

Chapter 6: The Thieves Way

stones would fall from nowhere when they passed under high cliffs. At night Aaron made sure to take the usual precautions. These seemed to work as there had been no further evidence of any creatures around the camp.

On the fourth day of travel, after a satisfying breakfast of cooked field mice on bread, Aaron removed the map from his backpack that had caused so much trouble back in the town and studied it.

"It should only be another couple of days I reckon," Aaron said. "We just got to follow this pass up into what is called the Flat Steps. From there, it is then just a simple trek across the plateau to get to the monastery".

Aaron pointed the way. The path before them led into a steep sided valley, above which tall cliffs rose several hundred feet or more on each side.

In high spirits after having made so much progress they started on their way into the pass. As they progressed, the cliffs began to close in until the valley was transformed into a steep canyon. Alongside the path, a stream lazily flowed in the opposite direction, giving the place a rather tranquil feel. Despite this, Luke could tell Aaron was anxious about something.

According to Aaron's map, without following the road this was the best way to get through this area. But still Aaron did not like this route and wondered if the road would not have actually been a better choice. But if the stories were true and the roads in these parts had been completely overrun by bandits then they were best avoided.

The route they were taking was known as the "Thieves' Way". Aaron had heard of this route before and knew that for a long time smugglers and thieves had been using it to transport their illicit goods from the rich far east beyond the mountains, thus avoiding the guard old checkpoints along the way.

As they progressed they could not shake the feeling of being watched; every so often a stone would fall and clatter its way down the canyon, re-enforcing this feeling.

"More creatures?," Luke asked.

Let's pick up the pace," Aaron said. Their speed increased to marching pace. This pace was as fast as they could go, partly due to their heavy packs, but mainly due to the loose rocky terrain that made up the canyon floor. Aaron had one hand on his bow, ready to strike at whatever might pounce.

The canyon floor ascended and the cliff walls closed in. They could tell they were reaching the end of the canyon as the walls were now barely forty feet high and the gap between a mere ten feet. The stream had now all but

Chapter 6: The Thieves Way

vanished leaving just a dried up shale bed in its wake. The canyon end was in sight a steep hill at the end marked the exit point.

Aaron stopped dead in his tracks. An arrow had planted itself deeply into the ground at his feet. A second arrow whizzed past, just missing Luke, instead it struck the cliff behind him before ricocheting off and spinning wildly across the canyon, were it finally came to rest on the pebbles of the dried up stream bed.

Chapter 7: Swindlers Bargain

Luke was shaking with the now familiar adrenaline flow, any moment another arrow could be loosed, and this time strike him. Luke dropped to the floor to find cover while Aaron did not move, he seemed as steady as a rock. An unknown voice echoed through the canyon.

"Well then, what have we here? Aaron! Is that you? You should have known better than to show yourself around here."

"Now, now, Jaroc old buddy. We are just passing through. If you let us pass, I may be moved to give you a few golden chits for your kindness."

The voice above them laughed at Aaron's statement. The voice quietened, and several hooded men armed to the teeth with bows, swords and even some with some kind of powder fired pistol revealed themselves above on both sides of the canyon. Two more men also began to approach from the end of the canyon, blocking off their escape in that direction.

"Why would I do that? A bribe?," Jaroc asked pretentiously. "All I need to do is to simply take it off of your corpse after I have had my men run you and your

Chapter 7: Swindlers Bargain

buddy through."

"Come on mate," Aaron replied. "What about old times?"

"Old times?," Jaroc repeated. "You mean that time when we robbed the nobles, do you? You know the one, the one where you knocked me out afterwards and took all my chits."

"So this is where trusting Aaron gets you?," Luke thought.

Aaron retorted, "Well to be fair you did have it coming. I know it was you who told the guards where to find me after the robbery. You just could not bear to let me have my share. I had to spend several weeks in that dismal hole before I could escape, all so you could keep all the loot we stashed for yourself. Robbing you back was the least I could do, Be thankful I chose not your life!"

"Enough," Jaroc shouted angrily. By now the two men approaching had reached Luke and Aaron with their swords drawn. Aaron withdrew his bow and readied it as Luke did with his dagger.

"Adam, One Eye, run these runts through".

The man with an eye patch attacked first with a war cry scream, his aim was at Luke's neck. Luke attempted to block the heavy blow with his dagger. It was successful to

Surface

a point, but the sheer force of the blow from the burly man twisted Luke's arms to his side and sent him hurtling face first to the floor. He rolled over quickly ready for the follow up blow. Floored, he was now easy prey.

Adam attacked Aaron with a thrusting motion, using his gladius style sword. Aaron blocked the thrust with the metal edge of his composite bow. As Adam reared back for a second attempt, Aaron used this time to loose an arrow into Adam's belly. Adam stopped mid-swing and staggered backwards before collapsing to the floor. The arrow had easily pierced his leather armour and his innards. Warm red blood began to flow from the wound into where the steam once flowed. Adam lay there; he was not yet dead but was screaming in pain and fear, knowing that death would soon be his fate.

Luke closed his eyes expecting the finishing blow to come; he knew his dagger would prove no defence now. The one-eyed man readied his swing, his sword held behind his back. He was ready to bring his broad sword straight down onto Luke's unprotected skull. Luke knew his skull, if struck, would splatter like a melon from the force of the blow. At least it would be quick, he thought. The man lifted his sword above his head and started to swing it downwards, towards Luke. As he did so, he saw Adam go down, felled by Aaron. In mid-swing, he quickly changed his stance and redirected the savage swing at Aaron in fury. However, due to only having one eye, he had the

Chapter 7: Swindlers Bargain

disadvantage of poor depth perception and the attack was way off the mark. This gave Aaron enough time to loose his second arrow of the fight, striking the man in the shoulder. The one eyed man dropped his sword as the arrow thudded into him and more blood joined Adam's in the riverbed.

The men above them aimed their weapons and pulled back their bow strings, ready to put an end to them once and for all. "Stop!!," another voice shouted. The owner of the voice sounded quite puffed and out of breath. "I have just just travelled from our Overking. I reported my sightings of these two, two days ago. The Overking wants them alive! I have been trying to signal you thus, yet you fell upon them anyway. The Bandit Overking, Traigon, shall hear of this."

Jaroc, against his wishes, was forced to order his men to hold fire. He had to forget his old rivalry, at least for now. Jaroc held his arm aloft, and the men released their aim, but they kept their bows and guns at the ready. Several more began their approach from the far end of the canyon. One of them stopped short of the pair, were he seemed to comfort the dying Adam. When the man stood up, Adam was dead. His throat had clearly been slit. The stream was now in full flow.

The man with the bloodied dagger was kinder to the one eyed man. Instead of killing him; he helped him to his feet.

Surface

The man, thankful, staggered away, being assisted by the man with the bloodied dagger. The other men withdrew their swords and poked Luke's and Aaron's back, indicating that they should get a move on. They were frog marched away.

The sun soon set, but the pace did not slow as they marched onwards. Luke needed to take his mind off of their situation and their rapidly developing blisters. Luke whispered to Aaron, "Bandit Overking Traigon, that is a bit pretentious, isn't it?"

"Well what did you expect him to be called, Bob the Bandit?," Aaron jokingly replied. They both felt a little better, so they spent much of the night telling jokes and trying to keep their spirits up, much to their captors annoyance, who would shout and prod them when they got too loud.

In the morning's painful light, with thirst gnawing at Luke and Aaron, they finally reached their destination, a large settlement. To say settlement, however, would be a poor description, it was more a ramshackle collection of shacks and tents. It did not look permanent, and Luke guessed the people there did not stay in one place for long. The iron doors opened as they approached and were marched inside. As they passed hut after hut of varying construction, Luke began to notice the absence of women and children. The few that he did see were in chains or

Chapter 7: Swindlers Bargain

doing some disgusting task.

Shortly they approached and entered the largest tent at the middle of the settlement. The tent had quite a simple interior, it was not stuffed full of stolen goods as one might have expected from a so called 'Bandit Over King'. Instead, the interior decoration consisted of an ordinary looking brown fabric floor and a few furnishings. The only things that were of note were the several ornate curved blades that hung down from two supporting beams of the tent and a few animal skins hung to the left and right on canvas walls. At least Luke hoped they were animal skins.

The Bandit Overking despite his pretentious name, sat not on a throne, but on a unpretentious wooden chair, preferring practicality to extravagance. A further curved ornate blade made of some brilliant white metal rested against his chair, and a leather whip hung behind his head. He was adorned with several golden items of jewellery but choose to wear chain armour rather than fine silks. His face bore many a scar of a tough life; his dark straight hair belied the probable darkness of his soul.

As they approached the Overking, stinging pain shot through both Aaron's and Luke's legs as they were hit with a cane from behind. This dropped them to their knees, and they were made to bow before Traigon the Bandit Overking.

Surface

"I should kill you now, Aaron," Overking Traigon said in a sombre voice. "Not only did you cross into our lands, you had the front to kill one of my men."

"It was in self defence!" Aaron protested. The guards around them readied, their swords drawn awaiting an inevitable order; they had seen this before.

The order they expected did not come, instead Traigon spoke more softly,"You should know I never ordered them to kill you Aaron, Jaroc took that upon himself, but you may have forced my hand, someone will have to pay for this."

"So, you will have us killed, Traigon?," Aaron asked agitatedly.

"Show me some respect you worm. It is Overking to you!" Traigon ordered.

"Sorry, Overking. What I meant to say was that I… our skills could be of some use to you."

"Well, funny you should say that as that does bring us to the heart of the things, which is why I ordered my men to bring you to me in the first place and also the reason why you and your friend are here instead of decorating the walls. I do have a job, a mission if you will, that suits a

Chapter 7: Swindlers Bargain

man of your particular talents. But first we have to deal with the events of the gorge as there is the question of discipline," Traigon mused.

Aaron remained silent, so the Overking continued, "Jaroc disobeyed orders and Grayson too, so they will be dealt with... So be it. Jaroc shall receive 20 lashes ... after slitting his brother Grayson's throat. It shall be Jaroc who shall suffer the most, Grayson's punishment would be brief in comparison."

The Overking looked at Aaron and Luke, who both could not cover their disgust. "Think me harsh, do you? Disobedience in whatever form cannot go unpunished, for there would be chaos if it did."

"Now as for you two?, he mused again. He then glanced at Luke before turning to speak to Aaron, "Do you need your friend? I would like to make an example of one of you two, as well. Obviously I need you, Aaron, but we don't need this... man do we?" He began to stroke the hilt of the brilliant white sword at his side.

After an all too long pause, Aaron replied to the Overking, "I need him. He is my partner in crime as it were, without him I would not be where I am today." Was he being sarcastic?, Luke thought as he looked at Aaron, who was crouched and restrained beside him.

72

Surface

Aaron continued "Why without Luke, it would be like having a bow without an arm to fire it with".

"Do not tempt me Aaron!," Overking Traigon scalded. Traigon then mused once again and in a much calmer voice stated, "Well, I suppose I could spare him, at least for now. The other two men's fate should serve as an adequate example. Know this," he turned to Luke, "They suffer and die in your stead."

Luke could not help but feel terrible pangs of guilt. Okay he owed Jaroc and Grayson nothing, less of nothing in fact as they had, after all, just tried to kill him. But because of him, and Aaron speaking up for him, one of these men had to die, and the other suffer a fate perhaps worse than death, to be forced to murder one of one's own blood, his brother no less.

Traigon spoke again: "Enough with this unpleasantness, back to the matter at hand". He paused for a second "Aaron tell me truthfully so that we may speak on good terms. With the route you were taking there is only one place you could be going. Do intend to visit the Monks of the Chalice?"

Aaron thought about his answer and decided it was probably best to answer truthfully. "Yes… Overking," he replied, not wanting to end up on even worse terms as bad terms would probably mean a slow and painful death.

Chapter 7: Swindlers Bargain

"Tell me then, for what reason do you wish to visit them?"

Again Aaron had to think carefully about his response. "That's simple, I wish to visit 'em to do what I do best which is to rob 'em of course. If it is a cut of the profits that you want then of course you can have fifty percent, I promise". Luke glared at Aaron, but Aaron owed the monks nothing.

"No, you can keep their trinkets for all I care, we have robbed them of plenty already. No, what I need is what they hold dearest, what I need is the chalice. It is the only thing that we have not been able to get our hands on thus far"

"But....," Aaron began to speak but was interrupted by the Overking.

"You are not going to tell me you cannot do this are you?," he said in a deep rumbling voice. He began to stroke the hilt of the sword again. Aaron remained silent and did not respond. The Overking cleared his throat as if he was about to speak until Luke decided to speak up for the first time. "Aaron can do it, sir. I have seen him fight and steal. He is both quick and nimble."

"Good", the Overking replied. "Guards, see to it that their possessions are returned to them, minus any chits they

Surface

carried of course."

Aaron whispered in Luke's ear while the Overking continued to bark orders. "Thanks mate, but the monks won't ever let us have it. I know they guard it well. I fear all you have done is delay our deaths... Oh well it should at least be fun to try." Luke did not reply. At this moment he did not like himself or Aaron terribly much. Aaron, the thief and killer, and Luke, the coward, he thought.

The Overking again turned his attention to Luke and Aaron. "Well then, you have your task, you best be going. Do not think about running away, for we will track you down anywhere you go. You shall also be provided with an escort to ensure that you reach your destination. When you complete your task, and complete it you shall, you will meet the escort again a few leagues from the temple."

The Overking looked at Aaron. He could tell his heart was still not in it. He spoke in a softer voice, "I am not an unreasonable man, Aaron. Succeed in this and I shall see to it that you are rewarded. Fifty golden chits, sound like a good bargain?" Aaron did visually perk up at the offer, though soon sank again knowing that he was not likely to live, let alone actually get the money.

One of the guards left and quickly returned with Aaron's and Luke's backpacks. The guard threw their gear at their feet. They barely had enough time to collect their

Chapter 7: Swindlers Bargain

belongings before being escorted to the gatehouse.

They waited in the makeshift gatehouse while the bandits debated who should escort them to their destination. Perhaps no one wanted to do this because Aaron had already killed one of their number? Or perhaps, more likely, it is just the sort of job that no one wants to do. "Babysitting," as one of the bandits put it, does not sound like a desirable duty. It took the bandits the best part of an hour to decide before eventually sending Luke, Aaron and their escort on their way.

Their eventual escort consisted of just two men, fewer than Aaron would have expected. The first man in the escort was a young man, standing just over five feet tall; he could have barely been more than fifteen years old. The second man was certainly much older than the first, his hair was greying. Deep wrinkles had set in around his eyes. He sported a short black goatee style beard, where the grey hairs had not yet taken hold. This showed that he might be ageing but still young enough to be handy in a fight, a fact backed up by a well-built body. Aaron studied them. He could probably defeat these two, but he knew if did he so, he would be tracked down forever more until his head sat atop a spike. This is what Traigon knew too, he thought, it was for this reason that two men were all that was required.

They journeyed out and in the daylight could see from

Surface

their position relative to the mountains that their earlier forced march had at least been heading roughly in the right direction. They were in the foothills proper, it would not be too far until they reached the plains of the Flat Steps.

Several hours of steep terrain followed as they headed in a south-easterly direction until they came across an uneven track. This track led through flatter terrain for a short while before taking them towards another settlement nestled at the beginnings of a canyon. Their escort ensured that they stayed well clear of this settlement, taking them off the path and up the steep sides of the canyon. However, as they climbed they got a good view of the settlement from above.

From what they could see this settlement sported the same colours as the bandit camp, except this settlement looked far more permanent. A wall surrounded the settlement like the bandit camp, but this time it was made from solid white stone, rather than loose panels of wood and sheet metal. Just inside the wall lay large white limestone buildings. These buildings made up the majority of the outer part of the settlement. Some of the buildings seemed to be carved directly from the large boulders that littered the canyon floor. The inner circle of the settlement contained large, multi-storey wooden structures, arranged in a loose circle around a central square. Luke did ask his escorts about the settlement, but he was told to mind his

Chapter 7: Swindlers Bargain

own business.

They continued to gain altitude and soon left the canyon behind. The temperature had noticeably dropped from before, and it also grew slightly harder to draw breath. The terrain eventually flattened again, so they paused and surveyed their surroundings. Looking back they could see the evening mists had shrouded the lower valleys and looking ahead they saw a flat featureless plain. The high mountains they had been chasing were now in full view at the far edge of the plain, stretched out across the entire horizon. They had reached the Flat Steps, and in the far distance a lone stone temple could be seen nestled at the foot of a mountain slope. This structure, Luke surmised, was their destination.

Night began to fall so they set up camp. There was no wood to gather for a fire, so they huddled in the warm clothes under makeshift blankets the bandits provided. The younger of the bandits stayed awake both to stop Aaron and Luke running off and to guard them all, from anyone or anything that might attack. Luke and Aaron were weary from the previous day's events and as they had not slept in the last two days; they quickly sank into a deep dark sleep.

Luke awoke and found it was still dark. He wondered what had awoken him, but only for a moment. As he crawled from under his tent, he could hear the sounds of

Surface

metal on flesh as well as other unidentifiable thuds and crashes. A fearsome battle cry broke through it all as if the cry itself would end the battle.

When he finally got outside he could see many figures moving and darting about at the edge of camp. With the only illumination coming from the moon, he could not get a clear picture of what was happening. He therefore stood up and moved towards the figures, getting a better look. Before him was an al-mighty fray. Several grasshopper like creatures surrounded the older of the two bandits. The bandit's sword swung wildly, severing mandibles and legs with every strike. Yellow blood littered the ground around his feet, from the constant gushing explosions of gooey blood.

A short distance away from the main battle was the younger of the two bandits. He was barely holding his own. He had slain one, but just as he was pulling his blade from the fallen creature, a second creature jumped at him from out of the darkness, knocking him to the ground, hard. Luke, if he wanted, could escape now; both bandits were distracted, he could make a run for it.

Something in him, maybe the guilt from the events earlier, prevented him from taking this action. Deep down he thought he needed to make amends.

He drew his dagger and started to run forward. His run

Chapter 7: Swindlers Bargain

became a sprint, and before he knew it he had dropped down onto his back and was sliding forward with his dagger raised upwards. He collided with the young bandit, pushing him out of the way and at the same time he thrust his dagger up into the creature's underbelly. The creature let out a squeal before it collapsed upon him, pinning him down.

The sounds from behind were dying down. The other bandit had slain most of the creatures, and was finishing the last one off before Aaron finally awoke and put an end to the battle when he loosed several arrows into the remaining creature. The creature writhed and shivered before dropping into a heap.

Aaron and the older bandit rolled the creature off of Luke, freeing him. They both looked down on him and smiled before helping Luke up. Luke then helped the younger bandit to his feet, where he still lay after having had the wind taken out of him by the creature's surprise attack and Luke's sliding kick. "Thanks, My name's Con," the young lad wheezed. "And this here is my father Geal".

Chapter 8: Whitevale

"Thank you for saving my son, Luke." The bandit seemed to warm to Luke now, although only slightly. Perhaps there was more to these bandits than simply being cold-hearted killers. Maybe they were, well human. Luke knew he would not get any more sleep that night and wanted to know as much as he could about these people. So, Luke asked them the reason why they chose to be bandits and how they came to be in the life that they now lived. To his surprise they told their story.

Luke learned that in a time just before Con was born that Geal and at least half of the bandits who occupy the region were once part of a wealthy farming town known as Whitevale. This town had managed to cultivate a rare spice that was unique to the region. This spice, known as Whitebazil, partly named after the town, is famed for having tremendous culinary powers. It is said that almost any dish can be infused with this herb enriching the flavour to new levels. The herb is also unique due to it containing high amounts of caffeine, making the herb quite addictive as well as flavourful.

They earned their living from trading with pilgrims and merchants who were going on to the east or coming back with rare meats requiring that little bit of extra flavouring.

Chapter 8: Whitevale

Rumours soon spread, and it was not long until people made the long journey east just for this spice alone. This brought the town enormous wealth, and with it the town expanded considerably. They even had to invent a whole new farming and storage method just to keep up with demand.

The news of this success bred jealousy from other places. They took defensive precautions knowing this, of course. They built a high wall and hired mercenaries, some of whom would become citizens themselves. One day the news of the wealthy town reached the bandits of the north. These bandits were a growing force in that region after the emergence of their new leader Traigon, who called himself, "The Bandit Overking".

He came to power after challenging the previous leader to a duel to the death. The leader refused and was then stabbed in the back by Traigon himself. He justified it by claiming that the previous leader was a coward. He proclaimed that now was the time for a new and strong leader. His main motivation for this move was more than just the lust for power and wealth. He believed in discipline above all else. He believed a disciplined army and work force could allow mankind to triumph over anything and everything. He wished to spread this ideal throughout the world. Except he could only do this with enough funds and the easiest way of getting funds, was from robbery and stealing. He changed the bandits from

Surface

disorganised loose alliance of thugs and mercenaries, into a military machine. With this might, he and his men made the journey south, spurred on with exaggerated rumours of wealth. Enough wealth to fund whatever he needed.

On a dark autumn's night, the bandit army attacked Whitevale. The battle was said to be a blood bath on both sides. The people of Whitevale held out and the bandits eventually had to pull back, having no real supplies except those that they could pillage. Out of jealousy some of the bandits decided to show their true colours and set the land alight burning the crops of Whitebazil. This showed Traigon that bandits alone were not the sort of people he needed for the new world he intended to create. After he had executed the group responsible, he hatched a new plan.

Despite the crops being lost and the knowledge that the town would be unable to generate any more wealth, Traigon reasoned that there should be at least enough chits in their coffers to use to hire a new, proper army and dispense with the bandit rabble. He bribed some of the mercenaries to leave the main gate unlocked one night. With that achieved they quickly overran the town.

Having seen the discipline and skill of some of the town's defenders, he gave those that survived a choice. Either join the bandits or they and their families would be put to the sword. No one chose the latter and Geal was one of those

Chapter 8: Whitevale

people. The women became the property of the bandits and the male children were trained and brutalised into becoming bandit soldiers themselves.

The failing in Traigon's plan was that the town had either hidden or spent all its wealth on things such as defensive precautions, new farming processes and fancy new buildings. This meant that with the lack of chits Traigon could not continue with his plan and hire a new army. He therefore had to resort to the small time robbing and pillaging of travellers passing by. The town became destitute and its populace was forced to live and work for the bandits if only not to starve. The small bandit nation as it had now become began to fragment as travellers began using different routes in an attempt to avoid the bandits, thus forcing the majority of bandits to move around from place to place. This is how life was now. Geal knew that that Traigon was not content with this and was hatching a new plan, but he did not know or say what this might be.

"Con is not my real son but he might as well be," Geal said as the sun's rays began to shed light on the landscape, painting it pink and orange. "He lost his father in the battles and his mother died in child birth. I took it on myself to raise him, rather then let those bandits corrupt him. I think I have done well, he is a good lad."

"So you were forced into this life?," Luke enquired.

Surface

"Alas, yes. At first I did it to survive. If Con had not arrived I probably would have just let them kill me, but now Con, he is my life. I live this life for him. I thank you again for saving him."

Geal decided now was the best time for a change of subject, "Anyway, we better get back. We could tell Traigon that you died in the creature attack, but he would require proof, such as your bodies. Instead, it is best to simply say that we escorted you to the temple. Whether you enter the temple or not is up to you, I will not stop you. If, however, you do still intend to go to the temple, it is only a few hours walk away now, and you should have no more trouble with those creatures during the daylight hours. May you stave off the long winters and may the summer winds bless your path". Geal and Con slowly collected their things and began to leave.

"Oh here, take this, I will say it was lost in the fight with the creatures". Geal took a short sword, bronze of hilt and white of blade from a concealed scabbard near his ankle. The brilliant white blade almost hummed as Geal removed it. It looked as if it was made from the same metal as the sword that Traigon owns. Geal tossed it, handle first, to Luke. "This is much better than your small, rusty dagger. This sword is sharp enough to cut through anything. Just don't go hurting yourself with it" he smirked.

"Here, how come I don't get 'out?," Aaron asked. Geal

Chapter 8: Whitevale

shrugged, which caused Aaron to mutter something distasteful under his breath.

The skies began to darken with clouds as they cleared up camp. "Well," said Aaron, "I heard what they said, it is up to us what we do now. But trust me, if you like living, there is only one way forward for us. That is to return to the camp, with the chalice. Well that or take up holy orders with the monks. What a bore that would be?," he joked.

Luke did not like either of those options and would rather have gone home at this point if he could have. He had already seen more violence and bloodshed in the past few days than he had in his whole life. However despite all that had happened, Luke still wanted to know about the children and what it is they wanted from him. So reluctantly he agreed in the hope of finding that out, and he and Aaron pressed on towards the dome shaped building in the distance.

Now they were on their own, Luke could finally ask how Aaron knew so much about the bandits and how he seemed to know at least one of their members.

As if sensing what Luke was about to ask, Aaron answered the question Luke had yet to pose. "Used to be one," Aaron said simply, before elaborating, "Unlike Con and Geal, I am not from Whitevale, I was instead talent spotted, as it

Surface

were."

"You see, I was young and felt quite successful with my thievery, I had been getting away with stealing for such a long time I thought I was invincible. I kept targeting bigger and bigger targets. Finally, I hit one target that was just too big and, well, I fell on my backside, both figuratively and literally. That story is best left for another time. Suffice to say, I was caught and chucked into a cell, probably to face execution."

"Only, as you can see, what with me living and all, I was not executed. Instead, the bandits sprung me. Apparently they had been keeping their eyes on me and seemed to appreciate my talent, something I think you should do more of Luke," Aaron half-smiled and winked.

"Anyway, at first the life of a bandit was a good life, It seemed so glamorous being known as a highwayman and I of course was grateful for being rescued. All the glamour was all tosh of course, and I soon found out the truth that they are nothing more than a bunch of murdering back-stabbers. I mean all of them, even those from Whitevale. It took some grizzly tasks and Jaroc's betrayal, who, by the way, is from Whitevale, to make me finally see what they all truly are scum. Honour among thieves, HA!"

"Is that why you killed Adam? Vengeance?," Luke questioned.

Chapter 8: Whitevale

"Well that was in defence, but basically, yes, I could not care less about them. Take last night. If you had not stepped in, I would have happily watched those creatures rip them apart. Sure they claim to be different, but trust me, they are not." Aaron looked up at the sky, "Oh well let's be off. It looks as if it is going to rain."

Before they did move, Luke posed Aaron a final question, "Does murdering them make you any better than they are?"

Aaron was actually quite annoyed by the question. If he did not kill them, then they would have killed him, simple as that, however, Aaron chose not to answer and instead he simply gave Luke a blank look. It was obvious he had considered the question, for he did not say another word until it began to rain almost an hour later.

Raindrops started to pound the ground, and before they knew it they were engulfed in a rainstorm. Luke enjoyed the experience. This was the first time he had ever felt cold raindrops on his skin and the wet breeze in his hair. He had never seen or felt anything like this rain storm before. Aaron, on the other hand, wrapped up tightly within his warm leather jacket and looked at Luke with a slightly puzzled expression, "Here, are you daft? Put your coat on, or you will freeze to death up here."

Surface

Luke at first ignored this advice, wanting to embrace this new experience further, however, it was not long until he relented, but by then he had already taken on the appearance of a drowned rodent.

They trudged onwards through the rain. Their clothes offered only limited protection against the elements, the rain seeped in through their clothes and their boots filled with water. Luke did not notice as he was already soaked.

Finally the rain and mist cleared, albeit momentarily,but this allowed them to get a closer glimpse of the dome shaped building that they now approached.

The building had looked to be of an uncomplicated design from a distance. However, close up it turned out to be of a much more intricate design. The dome was not really a dome at all; instead it looked more like a stepped pyramid, yet instead of being triangular it was circular in design. Below the dome colossal columns held it aloft. Large, stained glass windows occupied the majority of the spaces in-between those columns. These windows were decorated with various religious symbols, one of those symbols caught Luke's eye. He had seen it many times before, it was the hammer of the Hammerites. Surely a co-incidence he thought. Below and around the central dome were positioned more structures that made up the main working areas of the temple. Some of the buildings were of different colour and design and had obviously been

Chapter 8: Whitevale

added on over the years. The overall layout of the added buildings complete with the dome in the centre gave the entire structure the appearance of a giant turtle. The outer buildings taking the place of the turtle's legs, tail and body and the dome making up its shell.

They reached the main doors just as the rains came in again. The doors, made from a dark oak displayed no particular symbols or designs, except for the interlaced re-enforcing metal work around the wood. To the side of the doors Luke was surprised to see something familiar in this technological-lacking world. It appeared to be an intercom, that was of a remarkably similar design to the ones used in his home. Luke moved over to the intercom and Aaron followed.

Aaron looked puzzled at it, not knowing what it was. Luke pressed a button at the bottom of the panel and waited. He then pressed the button again and said, "Hello?" This made Aaron even more puzzled. Why was he talking to this thing on the wall? Finally after Luke pressed the button for a third time, an agitated voice replied.

"Go away!" it said.

At this point, Aaron backed off in fright obviously weary of this "magic" and seemed to want to heed the command. Luke spoke politely asking if they could be let in. He told them that bandits had attacked them and that they needed

Surface

some place to stay, even if it was just for the night.

There was a short pause before the voice in the panel spoke with a sigh, "Very well, you may enter." There were several clicking sounds as hidden locks and bolts slid away before the door itself shuddered and slowly swung open. Stood in the open doorway was a balding hooded figure.

The figure cleared its throat to speak, "You may stay the night, but you can stay no longer. We are weary of strangers; all too often you outsiders have taken advantage of our trust and our oath to help the needy, yet we still help you. Let no one say the monks of the chalice are not charitable," the old man under the frock said.

They were led inside and entered a large entrance hall, with two chandeliers hanging from the ceiling. Straight ahead at the end of the hall was another set of large wooden doors, again re-enforced with a metal lattice. Above the doors was a small window decorated with the familiar hammer design. However, this time the hammer was not alone, instead it sat atop a strange chalice.

Still dripping from the rain, they were led from the entrance hall through a door on the right and into a maze of almost bare corridors. They took several turnings, passing many doors and archways. "Well," Aaron said to Luke, looking back at the wet boot prints they were

Chapter 8: Whitevale

leaving behind, "at least we will be able to find our way back".

After traversing the maze for a while, taking several more turnings, they could hear noises that sounded like machinery that seemed to come from behind a locked door down one of the side passages.

"What is that machinery for?," Luke asked.

"Ah, so you are enlightened enough not to think of them as magic? Well then I shall tell you. That, my friend, is our mechanical forge. We make various trinkets that we can sell to the merchants who pass by on to the road to the south of here. We exchange these trinkets for food, water, essential supplies and nothing more. We care not for what luxuries these trinkets may fetch in other places. We have found, however, that others do care a great deal, and their greed leads some of them to try and take what we have from us by force. You will, however, now find that we have gone to great lengths to secure these trinkets and other items as of late. Let that be a warning to you if that is your intention."

As they walked on, they passed many more rooms, most of which of those that they could see contained very few furnishings. That was until they came across a rather intriguing room. The room itself was nothing unusual, however, what lay inside the room was. Arranged across

Surface

several desks were silver coloured boxes. Each box had a smaller box to the side. A dusty black glass panel covered the front of the smaller boxes. Luke recognised what these boxes were, they were in-fact computer terminals. The terminals were well laden with dust so had obviously not been used in a long time.

"Our library," the monk said after spotting Luke's curios gaze. "Unfortunately, the machines have not worked for a lengthy time." The monk gestured for them to continue down the corridor and so they pressed on. At the end of the next corridor, they finally reached their chambers, set opposing each other across the corridor. Both chambers contained a simple hay mattress, a wooden desk, a small fireplace and nothing else. The simple contents of the room, coupled with the cold, stone laid walls, gave the rooms more of an appearance of dungeon cells rather than places to stay. The monks, despite being technologically advanced, obviously lived simple lives.

Before the monk left, Luke tried to ask about the children but was simply told, "That is for the enlightened only". With that statement, the monk abruptly turned and left them in their chambers.

A different monk returned not long afterwards. He was kind enough to provide Luke and Aaron with dry clothes and kindling with which to light a fire in the hearth. The light from the fire gave Luke's basic room a far more

Chapter 8: Whitevale

cosier feel. It was not long before he fell asleep, after all he had not slept for the last two days.

Despite needing all that sleep he still awoke unusually early the next morning, the sun had barely begun to show itself above the horizon. He decided to investigate the computerized library he had passed earlier. As the monks remained silent, the only way open now was to see if there was any information on those terminals, after he had repaired one, of course. He needed to know about the children; it was, after all, for that exact reason he originally ventured to the temple in the first place. He would worry about getting the chalice later and was sure that Aaron was probably already taking care of it. So for now this was his priority.

The door to the library was not even locked, why would it be, after all the terminals were broken, what was there to protect? The monks seemed to know extremely little about this technology. Perhaps the terminals where a relic of a previous generation, the knowledge to maintain them lost ages ago, so they were considered useless junk.

Luke inspected the terminals; each terminal screen was blank and each refused to start. Despite this, a smile did appear on Luke's face as he recognised that the terminals were of a decidedly similar design to the ones he used and maintained in the colony. It must be all the dust, he thought. If they were this dusty on the outside, then inside must be far worse. Sure enough after removing the outer case from one of them he was confronted with years upon years of skin flakes, masonry fragments, dead insects and who knows what else. He blew away as much of the dust as he could. He then removed the components one by one, cleaning each one the best as he was able to without using nothing more than a simple cloth that he found abandoned in a corner. He then carefully and meticulously replaced and re-seated each component.

He did this with each machine, as each one still refused to start. He got to the last one. Maybe it was a bit of luck, or maybe he gave it that little extra clean, because he was successful, the machine booted. After several boot/start-up messages he was presented with a welcome screen entitled "Welcome to the Archives, may they enlighten your way." The title shortly disappeared to be replaced by a green and black heading list which filled the entire screen. Luke searched down the list until he found an entry that interested him. This entry was entitled "The children and Relics, a history".

Chapter 9: The Daring Theft

Unlike Luke, Aaron did not go to sleep that night; he had, after all, managed to sleep most of the previous night. He knew now was not the time for sleeping, for he only had this night to acquire the chalice that Traigon sought after. Aaron's first problem was finding it. He decided to approach this problem logically: "Wherever the chalice is," he thought, "it would be unlikely hidden away in some dusty vault; instead it would probably be out in the open for viewing and worship by the monks. Also seeming to be the foundation of these strange monk's faith, it would make sense for it to be... in the centre hall, of course."

Earlier Aaron had made careful mental notes of the route they took to reach their chambers. With these mental notes, he was able to retrace his steps. He darted from doorway to doorway every time he thought he heard a movement. However, all was quiet. He decided to go to the entrance hall as he surmised that the other large double doors led to the central chamber. After only taking one wrong turn, Aaron reached the entrance hall. He immediately tried the large doors quietly that led into the inner sanctum. No good they did not budge, locked perhaps? There was no obvious keyhole. He did notice something that looked like the sound box Luke used earlier at the entrance, but he did want not try it, for it might alert the monks. Aaron scanned the chamber, above the doorway was a small window with the hammer symbol on it. That is where he would try and enter; though the glass could be a problem. "One problem at a time, first how in the northern lands do I get up there?," he thought.

Aaron continued to scan the room with his trained thieving eyes. The next thing of note was that there were two beams stretched across above, a few feet below the ceiling. These beams held the chandeliers aloft. Continuing to search the hall, the only other thing he noticed was a large blue banner, imprinted with a golden hammer. The banner itself was held aloft by three large brass rings.

If only he had a few more days, he could have cased the place properly, worked out a plan. "Oh well, time to do what I do best. Make it up as I go along" Aaron said aloud.

Finishing his agonising search for anything of use, he returned to the centre of the hall, where the answer stuck out at him like the hand of a beggar, reaching out for freshly cooked unguarded pie. If he could get onto the beams he spotted, then it should be an easy walk across to reach the windowed opening at the far end. There was, however, no handy ladder or any obvious route up there, but being a thief this did not deter Aaron, he had a solution in his bag Mixed in with all the other tools of his trade was a rope, this rope he could use to throw over the

Chapter 9: The Daring Theft

beams and provide a means of climbing up there.

Except the beams were much too high for him to throw the rope. Every attempt saw the rope fall way short of the beam. However, maybe if he tied the rope to the end of an arrow, then the arrow could give him the extra height he needed, and the weight of the rope should stop it from embedding itself in the ceiling and drop the rope over the beam. He could use the free end of the rope to pull himself upwards. It would require strength, but he should be strong enough. Easy, he thought, with a smug smile at his own brilliance.

He lined up his shot and loosed an arrow. It did make it over the beam, however, the arrow slipped off the rope half way up before pinging off the ceiling and crashing down to the floor where the arrow splintered with a loud crack. He waited, he expected to hear cries of alarm; however, all he could hear was distant chanting from a possible ritual being performed. All else seemed quite. The walls thankfully were of thick stone and the sound luckily did not seem to travel far.

This, so far, was not his best work, and maybe it would not be as easy as he first thought. He lined up for a second shot; making sure that this time he doubled the knot over, to prevent the arrow slipping.

His aim was true and this time the knot did not come

undone. The arrow cleared the beam the weight of the rope ensured that it also cleared the ceiling, the trailing rope drooped over the beam. Almost before, the arrow had come down again, Aaron was already in the process of converting the other end of the rope into a makeshift harness. As soon as the harness was fashioned he started to pull on the arrow end of rope, hauling himself up in a sort of pulley system. As he ascended his arms ached more and more and by the time he reached the top, some 30 feet above the floor, his arms were in agony. If he were to give in now, he would fall to his doom on the solid floor below. With a great final effort Aaron managed to heave his body up and onto the beam. He knelt down panting, trying to catch his breath.

He did not give himself much time to rest and now focussed on the second part of his task, getting through the window at the end of the beam to access the hall beyond. Aaron noticed that the window had a hook on the outside, probably so that it could be opened at a distance. This was Aaron's lucky day, he merely pulled on the hook and the window swung open. "What luck," he thought. He retrieved the rope he had just used and then tied it off to the window's frame. He chucked the rope over his left shoulder and fed it around his back and between his legs before hooking it around his left leg. This enabled him to use the friction of his body to lower himself down the other side into the large hall safely.

Chapter 9: The Daring Theft

The hall that he descended into was remarkable. It contained many high tiered arches stacked upon one another. It was almost exactly the same as the hall he dreamt about back at the inn. There was one major difference though, this time there was no throne, only a pedestal, atop of which stood his prize, the chalice. "This must be what the children are guiding me to", he thought. But he also pondered the message about Luke and wondered what he had to do with any of this.

He approached the chalice. The body of the chalice was a brilliant silver colour, and its handles were jet black, possibly made from ebony. Upon reaching it, he could see that something was particularly odd. Yes, it was roughly shaped like a chalice, but it had no receptacle in which to fill with liquid, which is normally the main function of a chalice. The handles also appeared peculiar as they were distinctly square and not in fitting with the rest of the shape.

He examined the pedestal on which it sat, checking to see if there was some sort of mechanical or even magical protection. It had been all too easy up to now. After a lengthy examination, he could not see anything. He decided to, gently lift the chalice to see if anything would begin to trigger. He found that it was far heavier than he would have expected. As he began to lift, he noticed a small square in the pedestal underneath begin to rise also. "Ah, so it's a pressure trap," Aaron surmised. Aaron had

Surface

nothing with him to weight it down with, all his remaining gear was too light. He could not give up now, this close to his goal. He yet again used his thieving eyes to look around. Most of the floor space was used up by marble seats, arranged in a semicircle around the centre. They certainly were heavy, but were far too heavy and also attached to the ground. In fact, everything in the hall was either attached to something or was far too heavy to lift.

Racking his brain for a solution, he remembered the banner that he saw in the other room, in particular he remembered the banner's brass ring attachments. Maybe the rings coupled with the banner would be heavy enough? He went back to the main doors where his rope hung down. He was about to climb back up again when he noticed to the side what looked like another sound box. He decided this time he would risk it, it might actually be a mechanism to open the doors. Logically, the monks must be able to get in and out somehow.

He was right, part of the panel he pressed sunk into the wall and the doors swung open. It was however, a bittersweet moment as he realised he could have gotten in there without all this needless messing around with the rope if he had simply pressed the button! His face was red with embarrassment, he was glad none of his fellow thieves had seen this. They would have fallen off their chairs laughing at him.

Chapter 9: The Daring Theft

Back to business, he thought. He strolled over to the banner and pulled as hard as he could but it would not come down. The rings held it fast. Clank… he quickly turned around, startled. The doors leading to the main hall had closed by themselves. He was not too concerned though as he knew that the button would allow him access back into the hall again. "Well, I better check," he thought. He strolled back over to the doors and jabbed out with his finger to press the button, expecting it to offer little resistance and sink into a recess like the other. The button did not yield, though his finger did. Aaron did a mighty fine dance, holding his strained finger, cursing everything he could think of. After the pain subsided and he stopped dancing, he realised his plan to steal the chalice now was in serious trouble. His rope was on the other side of the door and he had no other way of getting back up there.

Would he give up? No, he liked having his head attached to his body. Aaron decided to leave that particular problem for now and returned to the banner problem. This was becoming more and more like a point and click adventure, good job Aaron had no idea what one was.

He noticed a catch on the rings. If he could hit that just right maybe he could bring the banner along with its rings down. He withdrew his favourite tool, his bow, and once again took aim at an innocent inanimate object. He missed. The arrow hit the wall just above the ring, but at an angle so acute it carried on with its journey travelling upwards before colliding with the ceiling. Aaron had to move quickly as the arrow came shooting straight back down, gunning for his eye. It clattered to the floor, This activity was proving to be extremely noisy, but what other choice was there?

It took several more attempts to dislodge just one ring despite every subsequent shot hitting the ring with a satisfying ping. The floor around Aaron was beginning to resemble a battle scene, arrows, arrowheads, bits of masonry and torn fabric, all now lay at his feet.

He now had only one arrow left. He had more in his room, but he did not want to travel back down the corridors for he might run into someone. He also needed to be quick as he knew the longer it took, the more likely he was to get caught.

Aaron pulled back on his bow as far as possible before he loosed his last precious arrow. It struck the target dead on with an almighty clang before splintering into a thousand shards of wood and feathers. Yet the banner still did not fall. Aaron grabbed the banner, to try yanking it again. As he grabbed it, it decided to fall of its own accord. It draped over and covered Aaron, while the metal rings followed and struck his shoulder. Good job too, because if the rings had hit the floor it would have made one heck of a racket,

Chapter 9: The Daring Theft

an advantage his sore shoulder cared not about.

He gathered the banner and wrapped it in a bundle around the rings. Now all he had to do was to get back into the main hall. He noticed a sound, faint at first but then he soon realised it was footsteps. The sound of clogs on stone grew louder, someone was coming. Quickly, Aaron examined the panel at the side of the door more closely this time. He spotted a small hole under the panel. "This looks like... yes, a key hole, now this is more my field." He reached into one of his many pockets and retrieved his second favourite tool, his picks. His picks were simple strips of metal, one pick was narrow and pliable the other pick was thick and ridged. These picks would be useless to most, but not in Aaron's skilled hands.

Quickly, he inserted his picks and began to manipulate the lock's innards. The lock soon clicked open, and the clear almost invisible perspex cover over the button slipped away, leaving the button unprotected. Aaron quickly pushed the button into its recess as the foot steps stopped just outside the other door to the entrance hall. The main hall doors opened, and Aaron quickly entered the main chamber before forcing the doors closed, just as he heard a monk enter the entrance hall.

Muffled voices revealed that there was more than one person in the room adjacent, either that or the monk was mad and was talking to spirits that were not there while also impersonating their voices. As of yet, the voices seemed calm. However, he knew that they would soon spot the missing banner and the mess that he had failed to clear up in his haste. Aaron withdrew his dagger and stabbed the panel hoping that this would somehow impede their progress. He would exit using his rope, still dangling from where he had climbed down earlier. It was then just a matter of hiding on the beam until things quietened down. His mind turned to Luke, what would happen to him? Nothing, he thought, as he had nothing to do with this. Even if they accused him, the monks did not seem like the violent sort anyway; no, they would likely just throw him out, Aaron surmised.

He ventured to the centre of the room and reached the podium on which the chalice sat, the voices grew louder and there was now a banging on the door. The monks now knew that something was amiss. "You in there, open up!" One of them shouted.

Quickly, he used the weight of the banner and rings to replace the weight of the relic. It was enough and the pressure pad did not rise. What Aaron did not know was that there was also a small electric current being passed between the chalice and two conductors on either side of the pressure plate. The cloth of the banner did not make for a good conductor.

The chalice dropped to the ground as Aaron's grip failed

Chapter 9: The Daring Theft

him, the world began to spin around him. He looked down at his thigh, barely able to focus, where he saw a small red dart embedded in his flesh, presumably fired from the trap he had just triggered. The world grew dark and cold, and he did not even feel the impact with the floor.

Chapter 10: Sometimes It's Best Not To Know

Luke's eyes scanned the on-screen document as he began to read. The children were first seen at the beginning of the Warm Age at around 13,401 AD.

"If that is the same date base as my calendar, then that is over two hundred years ago," he thought aloud before continuing to read on...

The children are said be the main driving force and the spark for the present day Hammer religion. The children are also considered responsible for the exodus of the first band of pilgrims to leave the underground cities. These people under the children's guidance began to build their brave a New World and came to be known as the pilgrims. These pilgrims would become the founders of all present day surface civilisations.

Many more colonists joined the pilgrims and together they continued to populate the outside world. The children had a role in all of this, guiding the people in developing their villages and towns, in that they taught them long forgotten irrigation and construction techniques. All the children asked in return for all this is that a small number of people must quest for holy relics. These relics, the children said ,would restore them to their

Chapter 10: Sometimes It's Best Not To Know

full potential and with their potential reached they promised to one day help the pilgrims to fully rebuild the world to the way it once was many millennia ago.

Augustus Branklin found the first relic in 13,459. It was the holy hammer and thus became the guiding symbol for the new religion founded in the children's name. The followers of this grand new religion came to be known as Hammers ,or Hammerites, after the first relic.

"So these monks are Hammers just like in the colony?" Luke pondered, but only for a short while, he read on;

In the year 13,493, some people began to stop believing in the children's word. They were never fortunate enough to see the children and came to believe that they were simply made up by people in power just so they could stay in power.

The non-believers eventually broke off to form their own civilisation. Without the children's help, these people struggled to survive and a great number, out of desperation and greed, decided to try and take what the pilgrims had been given by force. Spurred on by anger and jealousy they started a long and murderous campaign against the peaceful pilgrims. The murderers rallied more to their cause by saying that the pilgrims and their search for holy relics was foolish and that the children would not help mankind. Instead, they claimed that the children

Surface

would lead all of mankind to its doom.

The death toll was said to be catastrophic as they systematically slaughtered every pilgrim/Hammerite they found. The believers that survived the slaughter were forced to flee to the wild places of this world with whatever relics and technology they could carry. This temple being one such place they fled to; its strong stone walls kept out invaders. AMENDMENT: In present times the ills born against us who reside in these walls seemed to have been largely forgotten, though jealously for material wealth is still rife, and the world is not as safe a place as we would hope it to be.

Word of the slaughter got back to those in the underground cities, they sealed their doors in 13,505 for ever or at least the world was safe again. Today it is believed that the Hammers still have a strong presence in at least one of the remaining underground cites.

"So the slaughter is why no one was allowed out of the colony?," Luke spoke aloud to the empty room

He read on… *Once every decade the seals would be broken and one man or woman would be sent out. Often this person would actually be a non-believer, so that they would be safe from persecution. It was these people's job to gauge the current savagery and hostility of the outside world, they would accomplish this by simply living with*

Chapter 10: Sometimes It's Best Not To Know

the people on the surface. If they later returned alive to tell their tale, then that would mean it was a step in the right direction. How they choose these people, known as the "anointed ones," is not known.

Sometimes these people were given a more prominent task, to seek out and return one of the children's relics, the very same task or quest the first pilgrims were set with. Having no preconceptions, the anointed ones were often quite easy to guide in subtle ways without drawing attention to themselves. They would be led to one of the remaining relics that were sometimes located for safekeeping in the few small bastions of worship that are still present on the surface. It must be stated that the exact events that would transpire once all the relics are found is still not known; however, we must do this as it is the children's will.

"So this is the reason I was sent out! Am I one of these anointed ones? But I was caught trespassing, why send someone who is, in their eyes a criminal?" Luke could only barely bring himself to read on, he never expected to stumble upon this wealth of knowledge. He was, however, still none the wiser as to who these children truly were and what their motivations were. Luke had nearly reached the end of the document, there was not much left to read except a small section in a much smaller font at the bottom of the page.

Surface

AMENDMENT: This night I was visited by the children. The children claim that the chalice we hold is now the last remaining relic, to be collected. Upon the retrieval of the chalice by the anointed one, I am told the world will be ready to be rebuilt anew. The people in the underground cities can surface once more and with the children's help, they will lead mankind to a new golden age. - Head monk & archivist Lauren 06/05/13600.

"So this is my purpose?," Luke spoke aloud. "But I came here of my own accord, I was not told to come, was I?" He had to discuss this with the monks. Maybe if he told them who he was, then they would perhaps be willing to explain in more detail, at least better than some dusty electronic text ever could.

His path now at least seemed clear, though he could not shake the feeling of resentment, for being treated like someone's puppet.

Luke looked up from the console as he thought he saw something in the corner of the room, but when he focused his sight there he could see nothing, baring a couple of cobwebs. He returned to the text and decided to look for other information before informing the monks. He wanted to learn as much as he could in case the monks refused to give him information he needed.

"Let's have a look to see if there is anything on these relics"

Chapter 10: Sometimes It's Best Not To Know

he thought.

As he had finished browsing for the relevant topic, he saw something again and looked up. Where there was nothing but a moment ago a child now stood, the same child that had haunted him previously. The drum roll of his heart began to pound in his ears once more as before. The child again opened her mouth and again no words came. It was as if the child was trying to speak into his very soul but could not get through. His vision began to get smaller and smaller until it was as if he was stood at the end of a long tunnel, with daylight only a distant glimmer. He was going to black out again. Just as his head began to drop the child vanished, and with this Luke jumped upright with a startle. His vision cleared, though he would feel dizzy for some time. "Why are they doing this to me, I already am going to do what they want. Are they punishing me for something, or … trying to tell me something?," he pondered frustratingly.

Luke decided he did not want to stay in the room any longer and began to cautiously back out towards the exit, checking over his shoulder as he did, paranoid that the child might reappear. He just wanted to get the chalice and go home, put this whole thing behind him. But first he needed to convince the monks that he was the chosen one. He then realised he had a serious problem "Aaron!… he plans to give it to the bandits, no I can't let that happen. What would the children do to me then?"

Surface

He ventured along the corridor back towards the main hall, looking for the monks. It was not long until he came across one. The monk peered at Luke as if attempting to scald him with his vision alone; he was angry. The monk raised his hand to stop Luke in his tracks. The monk shouted, "You there! Go no further." The monk grabbed Luke's arm with ease as if he was controlling a disobedient child "Follow me!," he bellowed.

"So much for getting off on the right foot", Luke thought.

Luke was led the way he had come, passing his and Aaron's chambers. He noticed through the partly ajar door that Aaron's straw "bed" was empty and his belongings seemed to be strewn all about the place. Either Aaron does not like to tidy up after himself, or his room had been vigorously searched, thought Luke.

The corridor ended at a door with a simple plaque reading "Lauren – Head monk & archivist". The monk leading Luke knocked once on the door and after a short delay the door creaked open.

In the room revealed lay many books and scrolls, with the centre occupied by an old oak desk surrounded by potted plants. Sat at the desk was an elderly woman, wearing the same monk garments as the rest except for the colour. He garments were a deep red, which was of a stark contrast

Chapter 10: Sometimes It's Best Not To Know

to the beige clothing the rest wore. Her hair could not in reality be described as silver for it appeared to be more bleached white. It was arranged in a sort of bun, to stop the long hair getting in her eyes. Many age lines crisscrossed her face making her skin look like cracked, dried up mud. She had evidently faced many a winter.

Luke was directed to sit in the chair on the opposite side of the desk. She stared deep into Luke and with this stare the lines on her face seemed to straighten and grow shallower. She then spoke curtly, "We took you in, fed you and kept you warm. Yet you repay us by attempting to steal from us our most sacred relic? I see the world still has not changed".

Luke now knew for sure that Aaron had attempted to steal the relic and failed in the attempt.

"We caught your friend. He was actually fortunate that we found him as the trap he set off fired a poisonous dart that would have killed him if we had not treated him in time." She paused, looking at the slightly puzzled look on Luke's face. "You seem confused and wonder why we did not just let him die? We, unlike you people, are not savages. We are also not violent, we will never commit the crimes you non-believers do. So despite what some on the old council would demand, we will forgo your executions. We do, however, want you gone, immediately. You and any of your people will never return to this place as even we

Surface

have our limits, our doors are closed to you. Have you anything to say?," she said to Luke, as if telling off a school kid, Luke felt very small at this moment.

Luke had to phrase his reply carefully, he would have to tell the truth in a believable way. After all, he was lucky he and Aaron were not going to be executed, so he did not really want to push his luck. He must have paused for too long as he was soon hoisted to his feet ready to be dragged out of the room. He decided he had no choice but to get right to the point.

"I am the anointed one," he blurted out to a stunned silence "I came from the underground city, as you call it. I am here to retrieve the relic and to take it back with me." The silence ended with a sarcastic laugh from the head monk. Tact was evidently not one of Luke's strong points.

"You think we are stupid? You learned a bit about us from somewhere and thought you would try to fool us. Why should we believe you?"

"You are right, I did read about it in the archives, but…" Luke was interrupted

"The archives? No one has been able to access them for over five years!" She let out a small groan. She was certainly getting angry though she was trying to do her best to hide it and kept to her authoritarian tone.

Chapter 10: Sometimes It's Best Not To Know

"I did," Luke confirmed. "How else would I know that the children are the founders of your religion and know that you and everyone up here came from the... my world. How else would I know of the murderous campaign taken up to destroy the children's followers, the perpetrators would have certainly not advertised it! Finally, how would I have known that after the believers had fled underground, people like me were sent out, not just to retrieve the relics, but to learn if it would be possible for the rest of the believers to return. I know of the children's plans to..."

"Enough! You have made your point," the old lady, Head monk Lauren, said as she scowled and frowned.

The large deep frown on her face slowly turned to a look of puzzlement as she thought upon what Luke had said. "It's impossible, there is no way you should know that much detail. How did you come across all this information? Speak and do not just say from the archives!" She demanded.

"I cannot say otherwise because it is the truth! I repaired the terminal and accessed the information. I managed to do this as I have had to fix many of these terminals before." He paused for a moment before carrying on from that thought "According to your texts I am one of these anointed ones, perhaps the last one... so maybe it was the

… "children's will" for me to stumble upon on this information." Although Luke spoke the words, he realised he was not yet ready to believe them.

Her look of puzzlement deepened.

She seemed to be quite taken aback by this, perhaps she was ready to believe him. She mulled it over some more and spoke, "Indeed, only a person from the underground cities could do this now. I know of no other alive with the knowledge to fix that technology."

She slowly moved her index finger until it hovered over a button on her desk. She hesitated before giving in and pressing the button. Out of the desk popped up what Luke recognised as a microphone, into which she spoke. "Call in Relic keeper Evans, there is something we need to discuss."

Lauren and Evans questioned Luke for almost an hour, asking him every little detail about his underground city and what else he knew about the children down to the most minute detail. Finally, they questioned him about the Hammerites. It seemed that there were definite gaps in the monk's knowledge, probably lost generations ago.

For the last question Lauren and Evans got only frustration, as Luke knew hardly anything about the Hammerites, their secretive nature ensured this. However, they now certainly believed that Luke was telling the

Chapter 10: Sometimes It's Best Not To Know

truth. They knew now who he was.

Finally, the grilling was over and Lauren asked Evans to release Aaron to his chamber and to gather everyone else in the main hall. "We have a ceremony to perform," Lauren said.

Luke was led back down the corridors and through the heavy oak doors that Aaron so struggled with before. As Luke and Lauren entered the massive central hall they were met by a dozen other monks, who had already assembled. They formed a line with Luke and Lauren in the centre, and once formed they began to move towards the middle of the hall as one. As the line progressed, one by one the monks filtered off to form a circle around the plinth holding the chalice, with Luke and Lauren within the circle's centre. The monks then began to chant in a strange tongue. The chants started quietly at first, but soon grew louder and louder, eventually reaching a crescendo.

Lauren held up her hand for silence, and it was immediate. She cleared her throat and began to speak in her authoritative tone: "Fellow believers, we have amongst us the anointed one." Luke could not be sure, but he thought he heard a few gasps of surprise in the room at these words, despite the ceremony beginning it took those words to make them realise it was real, they had the anointed one among them. Lauren cleared her throat before continuing.

Surface

"Long have we waited for the people of the underground cities to find someone suitable to take this, the last relic, from its place of protection to a place far more worthy. As we all know, it is in this place the relics will be combined, and from this we will be led to a new, enlightened world. This is what the children promise."

"The children promise," the monks repeated.

Luke strangely could not help thinking that the last statement sounded more like a question, and maybe Lauren did not fully believe in what she was saying. Was she just going through the motions as if reading from an invisible script?

"This is a joyous occasion," she said quite blandly. "Luke, are you ready to take the chalice to its rightful place?"

Luke paused for a moment, "Am I?" he thought, but he spoke aloud "I am," almost as if, someone else was speaking for him.

Lauren slowly walked behind the plinth on which the chalice sat. She whispered some strange words above the chalice; those words seemed to resonate within the plinth. At first there was silence, nothing seemed to be occurring, but then there was the sound that was the unmistakable whirr of cogs spinning. This lasted several seconds before

Chapter 10: Sometimes It's Best Not To Know

stopping with one loud click. Luke guessed the words that she had spoken must have been some sort of password to disarm the trap that Aaron had triggered earlier. She strained but slowly picked up the chalice and handed it shakily to Luke.

"Please, gather your things. You and your friend must make this journey alone. We have taken a vow of non-violence so we can offer you no defence. With just two of you, you could pass unnoticed. If, however, you travelled as part of an entourage, then this would make you a target for the many thieves that prey on the roads along your route."

Luke only mustered, "I will go then," in reply. What else could he say? He could refuse but why? Doing this would enable him to be among his people again. Not only that, if the texts were actually true, then the relic combined with all the others could improve everyone's lot in life. Luke hoped that even if the texts were not true, the Hammerites in the colony would still think it was and would thus maybe free everyone who chose to leave their underground life, to help set up this new world.

Luke left the main hall and made his own way with the relic back to his quarters where he found Aaron sat on the straw bed, impatiently waiting for him.

"So I hear you have the relic. Great, the sooner we can give that to that almighty pig swiller, Traigon, the quicker we can get him off of our backs". These words that Aaron spoke brought the reality of Luke's situation crashing down, his feeling of purpose and destiny was instead replaced with a feeling of dread.

Luke just stared at Aaron as if he was a rabbit staring into a hunter's bow. No matter where he may have hopped the hunters arrow would still strike him. Luke had got so caught up in it all, he had forgotten about the deal they had made with the bandits. Luke was not going to let that deal stop him, his mind was made up. He must give it to his people. Doing so would solve all of his and his people's problems.

"We can't, Aaron. We must take it to my people" Luke said in a demanding tone. Up until this point Aaron was smiling however, with the statement Luke just made, Aaron too was overcome with dread, as well as anger, anger that was directed squarely at Luke.

"What, because of some mumbo jumbo prophecy? Yes, I listened in on that ceremony. You do not believe in that drivel do you? It's complete nonsense is what it is."

Luke replied now, getting quite angry himself.

"Whether I believe it or not is not the issue. My people do, and with this relic they may be free and, what's more, I

Chapter 10: Sometimes It's Best Not To Know

will be able to go home!" The other reason that Luke did not want to mention was the continued children appearances haunting his mind. If Aaron was not willing to entertain the prophecy, then he certainly was not willing to entertain the fact that the children were stalking Luke himself.

Aaron's anger grew, "If we don't give it the bandits, then Traigon will have my head. It is all right for you, no doubt you will get away and can forever sit pretty like a coward, in your underground bunker".

Luke frowned, "Listen, I am sorry. I have to do this, this is more important than me and you!"

"Tosh! Pig swill," Aaron spat "The only thing that is important in life or anything is the here and now not some stupid prophecy. Give me the chalice, Luke," Aaron demanded

"I can't, Aaron, I... I am sorry..."

Luke began to back slowly away. He knew and had seen what Aaron was capable of. On the other hand, Aaron had also saved Luke's Life, so he knew he was a good man. Hopefully, Aaron would just back down. But then Luke remembered the children had warned him about his eventual betrayal. Was this the moment?

Surface

Luke continued to back away until he reached the corridor, he then turned to walk away. In this time, Aaron's anger had boiled over and as Luke turned he leapt at Luke's feet, sending him and the chalice crashing to the floor of the stone laid corridor. Luke's left elbow took the brunt of the impact and the pain shot down that side of his body. Aaron made his way over Luke to reach for the chalice, which had landed just out of reach of them both. Whilst doing this, he made sure to pin Luke with his weight.

Now that Aaron was distracted attempting to grab the chalice, Luke seized the moment to make the first strike. He swung upwards with his free hand and struck Aaron on the left side of his jaw. The blow was not hard , but the surprise stunned Aaron enough for Luke to push Aaron off of him and grab the chalice once more. Aaron composed himself and grabbed the chalice too, they both struggled to wrestle it from each other's grip. Luke saw no choice but to strike Aaron again, and being above him allowed Luke to add downwards force to the power of his strike. His blow struck Aaron square on the nose splattering them both with Aaron's blood.

Aaron, being no stranger to a fight pushed the pain away and instead converted it into more anger and rage, rage he used to kick out with all his might, striking Luke hard and directly in the stomach with his knee. The force of the blow was so great that it pushed all the air from Luke's

Chapter 10: Sometimes It's Best Not To Know

body, Luke gasped for air like a fish out of water on the floor. Aaron let go of the chalice and stood up so that he was free to strike Luke again who was now lying in a prone position on the floor. He kicked him several times violently in the ribcage, sending sharp pains throughout Luke's body; there was a definite sound of bones cracking. Aaron finished his vicious assault with several more blows to Luke's stomach. These blows finally made Luke release his grip on the chalice.

Aaron stooped and picked up the chalice from where it lay. By this point, Aaron's anger started to subside and he struck Luke no more. "I am sorry it had to come to this," he said after he stepped over Luke's battered body. He began to gather his things to leave.

Like Aaron, Luke was certainly in a lot of pain. He tried to fight the pain off, but unlike Aaron, he had not the stomach for this sort of thing. Prior to leaving his old life Luke had never been in a fight. However, a sheer determination possessed him and along with the adrenaline flowing through his veins, Luke somehow, after what seemed like an age, managed to bring himself to his feet. He staggered into his room, at first just for some respite.

He was about to lie down, defeated on his straw bed. That was until he saw the hilt of his white bladed short sword sticking out of his bag, inviting him to use it. Luke could

not believe it had come to this, and with his last bit of
adrenaline he charged, sword drawn, at Aaron's back
while he was still packing his things. At the last second, he
hesitated and instead of running him through he brought
the blade past Aaron before bringing it back and holding
it at his neck. Before Aaron could react, Luke used his own
body weight to pull the startled Aaron to the floor.

"So you will kill me? Do you know what that is like to kill
someone, Luke?," Aaron questioned.

"I don't want to" Luke's arm was now shaking violently.
Could he kill a man? There was a lot at stake. He could not
stop a tear rolling down his cheek. He felt Aaron's warm
blood, dripping down onto his hand, Aaron's nose was still
bleeding heavily. "What am I doing?," he thought, "This
man had saved my life, probably more than once."

"There must be another way", he said softly almost under
his breath. Slowly, Luke lowered his sword before
eventually withdrawing it altogether. Aaron thought
about taking this opportunity to take Luke's sword and
strike back and kill his companion. However, he too felt
unable to do this. He no more wanted to fight Luke, than
Luke wanted fight him.

Aaron instead, simply said, "Well, I am all ears, unless you
decide you want to cut one off." Aaron always tried to
make light of grave situations as, more often than not, he

Chapter 10: Sometimes It's Best Not To Know

got himself into grave situations. However, he did speak his next sentence in all seriousness, "It's not just the fact Traigon would hunt me down. It's those chits he promised, I need'em." Luke's eyes rolled at this statement.

"You misunderstand!," Aaron shouted before going on to say in a quieter voice, "I would not just use 'em for me. Have I told you about me family before? Those fifty golden chits he offered, would change their lives, allow 'em and me to live a life that is worth living, rather than in poverty in a backwards farm."

Luke was beginning to feel guilty, he could see why Aaron fought so hard to claim the chalice. What had happened to Luke to make him almost willing to kill this man over a silly shaped cup? He then started to think that maybe Aaron should have the relic. But he too so desperately required it, if only there was a way they both could have it. As impossible as the idea seemed, he began voice an idea that had not yet formed, "We obviously both cannot have the chalice, but what if… hmm… but how?"

"The forge! Of course," he spoke aloud to Aaron. In his excitement he moved a little too quickly and he felt a sharp pain shoot through his rib cage, but this did not deter him from continuing to voice and formulate his idea. "Aaron, the monk's forge, we can ask the monks to make another one, a fake chalice. We will say it is to divert potential thieves. This would mean the bandits can have the fake one and we give the real one to my people. That way I would get my people's freedom and you would get the money to support your family."

Aaron mulled it over. It was a good plan, but he would have preferred it the other way around. He did not like the idea of giving a fake chalice to Traigon. But he dared not risk arguing with a man with a drawn sword, and it was a plan at least.

Luke sheathed his sword and a long silence settled over them until Aaron looked at Luke, now holding his chest.

"Luke, I am sorry about your chest, I gave you quite a battering," Aaron said.

"Sorry about your nose," Luke laughed jokingly in return, but he had wished he had not as even sniggering caused him to bend over in pain.

"You really did a number on me," Luke said.

"Rest, mate" He handed Luke the chalice. Luke was surprised Aaron could trust him with it after what had just happened, though neither of them were in a fit state to fight for it again. "I will go and get the monks, just as soon as my nose stops bleeding, and we can outline our plan."

Chapter 11: Bandit Loyalties

For several days and nights the monks worked the forges hard to produce this new, fake chalice, believing its purpose to be a mere decoy, should anyone confront them. Unknown to all parties though was that this fake chalice was destined to make as much of an impact on people's lives as the real thing would have.

Luke was grateful for the rest he gained from the forging. He needed time to recover as Aaron's will to take the chalice from him had been strong.

They both tried to put the incident behind them, which was a task far easier for Aaron as he had no lasting injuries to constantly remind him of what had happened. All too often an awkward silence prevailed between the two throughout the time they remained at the temple. Aaron did try to break the silence a few times in attempt to perk up Luke's spirits, but jokes like, "You crack me up you do, no wait, I did that to you… sorry about that," did not go down that well.

After a week the time had come for the monks to present them with the new chalice, which was of vast relief for Luke as he was not sure how many more "rib" jokes he could take from Aaron.

Surface

The craftsmanship of the new chalice was remarkable; there were no discernible differences or markings to differentiate it from the original. If Luke and Aaron had not been told it was fake, they would not have been able to tell the difference except maybe for a very slight different tint of the metal colouring, which was the only thing the monks were not able to fully replicate, even with their remarkable craftsmanship skills.

The plan was not entirely to Luke's liking as he had failed to persuade the monks to take the real relic to his people. They would not agree for it was the anointed one's task alone, to perform. A compromise was brokered, however, and the monks reluctantly agreed to take the real chalice to the market town of Archesh, deep within the gorge where Luke awoke from his slumber a month earlier. This town was a place of worship, it still housed a small group of believers. Archesh does not have the massive walls to protect it like the temple, it instead relied upon its sheltered position, and its secrecy. Not a perfect place, but it was not only the best available, it was the only place possible along their route.

So the plan was set, the monks would take the real chalice to Archesh while Luke and Aaron would transport the fake chalice as a diversion, though the monks knew nothing of their plans to deliberately hand it over to the bandits. If they knew that part of the plan it probably would have destroyed the little trust they had built up

Chapter 11: Bandit Loyalties

with the monks thus far. They simply instead would claim it was stolen from them when they arrived in Archesh. From there, Luke would ferry it along to its final destination, his home, the journey from Archesh to his home being acceptedly safe.

They did not set out immediately as Aaron persuaded Luke, much to his annoyance, to let his injuries heal for the long journey ahead. The monks turned out to be quite a bit more hospitable than how they first appeared as they did not seem to mind the pair staying longer. They also never enquired upon how they came to be afflicted with their injuries while within the sanctum of the temple.

As time went on Luke's injuries healed more, and his ribs went from constant throbbing to just a pain when he laughed or ran. Aaron seemed to delight in telling jokes, just to hear the laughing followed by "You are a total pig's ear, Aaron!". In total, they stayed almost a month, several weeks longer than they initially expected. But even the friendliness of the monks could only last so long, so when the monks hospitably started turning to hostility they finally decided it was time to head out.

They left at dawn. The sky was a deep red crimson, as though a bloody battle had played itself out throughout the heavens. As they began to leave the temple behind they could see several shadowy figures following them before veering off in a different direction, the real chalice was in

Surface

their hands now. Luke hoped it would reach its destination safely.

The red dawn was soon replaced by clear blue skies of the morning and the air was crisp. This was in contrast to the day of their inward journey where cloud and rain had blocked their view. They now had a clear view of the landscape around them as they crossed the plains. The view was rather monotonous, however, as it consisted of flat, dark green, grassy plains, almost as far as the eye could see. Only the splendour of the mountains behind them broke that monotony.

They crossed the plateau for most of the morning, this caused Luke's ribs to begin to throb again. Finally mid afternoon they approached the end of the plains to Luke's relief. The grassy plains seemed to just end, giving the impression that they were about to walk off the edge of the world, but when they got there they could see a steep grassy slope dropping down.

Over the edge, they began their descent. At this point, the view was like that of an eagle soaring majestically over the land. Immediately below them was a stark mountainous terrain, the terrain they climbed over weeks earlier. It almost seemed impassable with its many limestone valleys and sheer cliffs. Beyond that the terrain steeply descended away again, before becoming gentle rolling hills which stretched off into a distance haze. On those hills, they

Chapter 11: Bandit Loyalties

could make out a patchwork of meadows and small woods that were dotted in between by what looked like buildings. On the horizon to the right, mixed in with the meadows stood a large single snow capped mountain that seemed to jut out almost unnaturally from the landscape. Luke realised that his home lay under that mountain.

As they got lower they regained the trail they took all those weeks ago. The bandit camp and Whitevale were now visible, no longer blocked by the land. In just a few hours, the bandits in the camp would spot them, meaning that it was only a short while until they found out if their plan would work.

No one had spoken that day until Aaron finally decided to speak. "You know mate, if this works out, we will have everything we need, which means we may as well part ways. I mean we will have to, you got your other life and I have my family. I know what you are thinking. It has been way too much fun to stop now, but you know what they say about too much of a good thing, eh?" Luke nodded understandingly.

However, Luke was strangely saddened by this announcement. He found this strange, not only because Aaron tried to make a batch of spare ribs out of him, it was also a fact he really could not trust him, even more so since their fight. Maybe Luke had strangely grown to like him? The main thing that truly saddened and well scared him, was the realisation that he would be left alone in this savage world to fend for himself should Aaron leave before he returned home. Home, he was going home. He never thought he would miss it so.

They continued to press on and soon they neared the bandit camp. In front of them up the path a lone figure approached; they had been spotted as expected. Just short of being in view of the camp proper they met the figure, that figure was Con. He waved, directing them to stop before quietly making his way over to speak to Luke.

"I have not told my father I was going to meet you here. I wanted to know if you were successful as our Overking... Traigon grows inpatient. You are only one of a few people other than my Pa that were ever kind to me out here, and it is because of that I wish you had simply fled. If however, by some miracle you do somehow have the chalice, I reckon you should have nothing to fear, just don't let him cheat you. Know I will be at your side if you need me."

Luke revealed the chalice from under his clothes for a brief second and Con smiled softly before quickly turning tail in the direction of the camp to report their arrival.

Prompted by spotting the chalice, Aaron held out his hand "Best let me take that, it would look strange if you were to hand it to him," Aaron requested. Luke hesitated at first, but remembered it was a fake and so duly handed it to

Chapter 11: Bandit Loyalties

Aaron.

Several men filed out of the camp and walked into view before many more joined them, the lead man was Traigon himself. He strolled out towards them under the fading late afternoon sun, flanked just behind by several men on each side. Traigon, unlike last time, certainly now looked like a "OverKing". He was wearing both his sword and whip and was dressed in all kinds of fineries. Perhaps he was putting on a show of power.

"So, is it true? Do you actually posses the chalice?" He showed a beaming smile with a hint of malice "Of course you do, why else would have you returned? Well, I must say I am impressed. Hand it over then," the Overking requested, almost politely.

Aaron removed the chalice from inside his backpack where he had placed it but a moment ago. The chalice glinted in the late sun, perhaps for the last time before coming into possession of the dastardly so-called Overking, probably to be locked away as a trophy or bartered away for slaves. Though it pained him to do it, Aaron knelt down on one knee and formally presented it to the Overking. It was immediately snatched from Aaron's hand, and the Overking smiled again before the smile turned to a grin, a grin of victory.

"Yes…," he said, "The children did foresee this for me.

Surface

From now on I shall not just rule Whitevale, I shall rule and bring order to the whole of the Southern realm. You see Aaron, they told me that someone one day would be able to bring me the chalice, little did I know that someone would be you."

So maybe that dream I had was true Aaron thought the children do indeed lead people to treasure and riches.

The Overking continued with his monologue, interrupting Aaron's train of thought,"You may not know what you have just given me, Aaron. Did you know the power of this is enough to command respect and obedience of any man? It is the ultimate tool for discipline. It is also said that it will empower the wielder to create a portal to travel great distances in an instant. With this, any settlement would join my rule. Think of it Aaron, with this we would no longer need to rob and pillage, I could see my will done all over without resorting to brutality and bloodshed. Aaron bringing me this has saved a lot of lives, you should be proud of yourself."

Traigon held out a purse of golden chits, "I have no issue giving you this, I reward those who do well. But it is most likely that after I use the chalice you will gladly return them to me."

Despite what he just said, the Overking's hand still hesitated just outside of Aaron's grasp. He then withdrew

Chapter 11: Bandit Loyalties

his hand, obviously he actually did have an issue just handing Aaron the chits. "Nice try Aaron, I will test it first. I have, after all, never actually laid eyes on it and have only seen it in drawings. This may just be a decorative ornament for all I know." Aaron's and Luke's faces were noticeably red as Traigon held the chalice aloft as if expecting something to happen, but alas nothing happened, silence.

Aaron, of course, knew full well that even if what the Overking had said was true, nothing was going to happen with this particular chalice. Why did the monks not mention it was supposed to have mythical powers?! Aaron would need to think of a plan and quick, for he and Luke were about to be in highly troubled waters indeed.

Traigon tried again, but it had the same result. The malicious smile that had been on his face until now quickly turned to an angry frown. With a nod of his head and before Luke and Aaron could react, swords were placed at their throats.

"Well," the Overking said in a remarkably calm voice, for he did not have the look of a calm man. "Either two things are true, either the children lied to me about its power or… or this is a fake. The children have not led me astray so far, so the latter is most likely true. So, Aaron, where is the real one?"

Surface

Luke's and Aaron's backpacks were removed and searched before their gear and supplies were passed about the men until only the empty husks of their packs remained, which were unceremoniously dumped back at their feet. However, in their haste in searching for the relic, they had not yet disarmed Luke and Aaron, but nevertheless they were powerless to use their weapons.

Yet again Luke was in a situation where death seemed imminent. He was not sure his nerves could take any more of this as his heart began to race. The effect worsened when the Overking then said, "Well then, Aaron? Or should I kill your friend for a bit of motivation?"

"There is no other, how could there be? What you hold is it," Aaron protested falsely.

"Lies!" The Overking was no longer speaking calmly. "I say it again! Tell me where the real chalice is." Luke shot a glance at Aaron, wondering what he would do, but Aaron did not answer the Overking.

A sharp pain shot through Luke's neck, and a small trickle of blood started to drip down the sword and then onto the earth. Another bandit rounded to the front of Luke. Before Luke could see who it was he was struck in the face. Red and white fairies danced in his vision from the impact.

The Overking nodded and that same bandit withdrew his

Chapter 11: Bandit Loyalties

sword and aimed it at Luke's belly. Aaron did protest at this point, but he did not reveal the truth of the chalice's location. "Enough" Luke was thinking, "the chalice is not worth my life". "Tell him," Luke called, but Aaron remained silent, would Aaron really let him die? Why? What would he gain? Luke did not find out.

Twang! An arrow streaked through the air before coming to a sudden stop in Traigon's side. Traigon's eyes widened, startled by the sudden trauma. He staggered sideways, clenching his side. The bandit with the sword currently aimed at Luke turned and ran towards the shooter. A second arrow was loosed, this time an even more deadly precision than the last, piercing Traigon through the neck. He immediately fell to the ground, where he writhed and squirmed. He gargled the words "but the children promised..." before a rush of blood garbled his last words. He let out a death rattle before he writhed and squirmed no more.

A man ran just outside of Luke's vision, to his right. Luke's head was still held over a sword, and he could not twist his head to see who it was. All he could do was listen to the sounds of running and yelling and several more "twangs" and "swooshes" as arrows were loosed all around him. A deathly scream of pain came next, followed by the sound of metal on flesh, stopping the screaming mid-flow. With this, the fighting became even more frantic as more seemed to join the fray and soon no more distinct sounds could be heard except for the words: "My son!" which was bellowed above all else, including gun fire.

The bandit holding Luke and Aaron let go to join the fray. Aaron and Luke were now free to see the carnage that was occurring all around them. Geal was at the centre of it all, again surrounded by enemies on all sides. He would soon be overwhelmed as more ran into the melee and entered the fray. To Luke and Aaron's surprise many of those who ran in did not attack Geal, but instead they began hacking away at his assailants.

"For the White Vale!" they cried as more of them crashed into the bandits attacking Geal. The bandits were also re-enforced by a surge of bandits pouring out from the camp, and the melee turned into a full-scale battle, with all the chaos that implied. Aaron loosed several arrows into the fray. Luke wondered how he knew who to aim for. Or was he not aiming at all? Red jets of blood sprayed in every direction as arrow, axe, sword and shot met their targets. It was impossible to tell who was winning and who was losing.

Luke just stood there watching it all, unable to look away, that was until three bandits broke off, at first to flee, but upon seeing Luke and Aaron they changed direction and charged at what looked like easy targets. Luke began to back away as Aaron stopped one with an arrow to the heart, felling the man instantly. However, he did not

Chapter 11: Bandit Loyalties

manage to stop the second one as he nimbly swerved away from the arrow. The second bandit leapt into the air and brought his massive war axe down to strike Aaron. Luke turned away, not wanting to see the results; he was too far away to help. He heard a loud crack and a scream; the blow had hit. Luke could not help himself. He turned to see the damage, but he could not see how Aaron faired as his attention was now drawn to the third charging man, who had reached him and was trying to behead him.

All of his concentration was now on this moment, this one man in front of him who was trying to end his life. The sounds of the battle faded away until all he could hear was his own pounding heart and his frantic breathing. Luke in that moment subconsciously took in all the details of the moment at hand. He noticed the details of his opponent, like the length of the black stubble around the man's chin and the rough cut of his hair, the smell of the man's mead filled breath and his look of utter anger and hatred. Time, it seemed, had almost stood still in this moment as the man brought his axe around wildly towards Luke's neck. Luke felt he had all the time in the world to react, but his body did not seem to want to move quick enough.

Still, Luke managed to move his arms in time and quite artfully blocked the blow and the several subsequent blows, Luke was surprised with himself, but how long would he last against this? The man struck again, Luke blocked again. After each strike and block the man got angrier and struck with even more force. Luke knew he would not be able to keep this up forever. The man reeled back to strike down on Luke again, maybe for the final time. Luke saw an opening in this wild attack and before he knew it his long, white dagger was now embedded under the man's shoulder. Luke withdrew his dagger and could see that its once white blade was now as red as the hole in the man's side. The man fell immediately, dead.

Luke was now operating on pure survival instinct. He rushed over to Aaron to strike at his attacker. The man blocked the blow, knocking him back and off balance. As he staggered back, he got a good view of Aaron and was glad to see he had no visible injuries. The blow he had heard earlier must have just been a glancing blow. Aaron was losing the fight though. He was falling back trying to block blow after frenzied blow, his counter attacks constantly missing their marks. His usual precision seemed lacking. However, now with Luke's help, they gained the upper hand and succeeded in pushing the man back. Now that Luke was facing the man he could see that he knew him. It was Jaroc, out for revenge, no doubt.

Jaroc continued his wild swings, despite being on the back foot, until finally one struck home, slashing deep into Luke's right arm. The pain was severe. Even with all the adrenalin coursing through his veins he was unable to swing, his arm also felt limp. So he took a leaf out of Aaron's book and kicked Jaroc in the stomach knocking

Chapter 11: Bandit Loyalties

him backwards before he then stumbled over a rock. This gave Aaron the opportunity to drive his dagger into Jaroc's shoulder, forcing him to drop his weapon. Jaroc grunted, but managed to continue fighting, even though he was now attacking with just his bare hands. Together Luke and Aaron stopped his attacks and forced Jaroc to the floor. Jaroc held up his arm to protect himself as Luke bore down on the man with his dagger held in his other hand, ready to kill. Luke, however, could not do it. Flashes of the other man's dying face now started to fill his vision. Jaroc used this moment of hesitation to scurry backwards before getting to his feet and fleeing. Luke expected Aaron to stop the fleeing man with an arrow from his bow, but he did not. "I thought Aaron hated this man," Luke thought.

Luke stared at Aaron, and it soon became clear why he did not loose an arrow. Aaron's bow had been cleaved in two and lay broken at his feet. Next to his bow there appeared to be several small sausages, perhaps Aaron's pack had been ripped open in the fight. But then he remembered that they had all their supplies taken from them. Luke stooped down and upon closer examination Luke was horrified to learn that those sausages were in fact fingers, Aaron's fingers.

Aaron must have lost them in an attempt to block the first blow, a blow so savage that it cleaved his composite metal and wood bow in two. His fingers must have still been gripping the outer edge and were hacked off as if

Surface

butchered by a cleaver.

Aaron also now stared at what was on the floor. The look of horror and pain crossed his face as realisation of what just happened was finally allowed to come to the forefront of his mind. He stood there as if his boots had sprouted roots. He was planted on the spot in the middle of the battlefield.

A man spotted them from the fray and thought that they might be an easy target, so he began charging at them, having just slain his previous foe. Aaron seemed to be in a daze and looked like he would not react. Luke also was in trouble. His mind and body were almost spent. Luke did his best to hold his dagger ready, feebly awaiting the man's onslaught. He knew that one way or another it would soon be over, he could rest. The man stopped several paces short; the reason was immediately apparent. A sword had burst its way through his chest, Geal's sword. Geal had slain all those attacking him and was killing everyone else who was not on his side. Geal kicked the man from his sword and proceeded to turn with bloodied anger to the next man who dared approach.

It was becoming clear now who belonged to what side, bandits on one and conscripted people of Whitevale forced into banditry on the other. What was also becoming clear was that the people of Whitevale were winning the day. It was not long until there were only a

Chapter 11: Bandit Loyalties

few hundred bandits remaining. Those few hundred began to flee in all directions, a few back to their camp only to be cut down, while the majority fled in the direction of Whitevale, hoping to find allies there in the corrupted garrison. They were pursued and the fight moved away towards Whitevale, both sides still had a foothold there.

Luke and Aaron were soon alone aside from the corpses. They did not follow the battle and instead remained where they stood, not knowing what to do, perhaps they were in shock. They were both finding it hard to even stand. They swayed on their feet trying not to fall onto the bloodied ground. As night began to fall smoke could be seen filling the horizon; the fires in the distance were making the sky orange and red, Whitevale was burning.

Chapter 12: Ellana's Warning

Aaron did snap out of his stupor, long enough at least to do his best to stem the bleeding from his fingers with his intact left hand before seeing to Luke's arm. "We will be okay mate," said Luke to Aaron, trying to reassure him as he bandaged his arm. The words, however, fell flat as even Luke did not believe his own words. With the injuries treated, in a manner of speaking, they slowly made their way from the battlefield, not wanting to loiter in this graveyard any longer.

They had barely gotten a few hundred feet from the battle before they both collapsed in a ditch through a combination of both exhaustion and their injuries. Their bodies wanted to shut down, yet for Luke he could not rest. All he could do was envision the face of the man he had killed and the image of blood dripping from his dagger. This mental self torture went on for some time until finally another vision began to creep in. The image in this vision was blurry and undefined at first, but it soon revealed itself to be a face. The face, however did not belong to anyone who took part in the battle. It was instead the face of a child, a child he had not seen before. This was a boy who looked barely ten with freckles, ginger hair and a smile. Unlike his previous meetings with the children, the cynicism was absent in this child's face as

Chapter 12: Ellana's Warning

was drum roll in Luke's head that normally accompanied the appearance of the children. Perhaps he was merely dreaming.

Luke soon began to feel a warm glow, something else he had never experienced in an encounter before. It felt as if he had just settled next to a fire after a long cold day on the road travelling. The world, along with any visions of the battle that haunted him, soon left him behind. He realised he was not outside any more, instead he stood in a strange room, the walls of which seemed to shift and shimmer. If he looked away from one area of the wall and then looked back, that section of the wall would be a different colour. It was as if it was shifting in the corner of his eye. The walls and floor appeared translucent, yet he could not make out what lay beyond. The whole effect made it look like he was peering out from inside a giant bubble caught in the sun's rays. He was not alone for there was a child in front of him who now held out his hand inviting him to grab it as if welcoming him. When the child spoke it was not a voice of a thousand people, no, this time it was the voice of a child.

"Your people are strange, why do they fight over our relics?," the child asked almost innocently. Luke did not reply. As if to illustrate the question, one of the walls shimmered and faded away to reveal the bloody scene of Whitevale. There was panic in the streets, brother was killing brother. The once grand settlement was being

Surface

destroyed.

Luke looked away and the window closed.

"You're hurt, both here," he pointed at Luke's shoulder, "and here," he pointed to Luke's heart. The child continued to offer his hand, Luke hesitated. The child just smiled. In the end Luke relented and took hold of it. As he did he felt a rush of reinvigorating energy course through him, returning his body's energies. The child then spoke, "You are brave in what you are doing to help me, and my kin, I only hope that, in the end you are strong enough to do what is right, for we may not be." With that the strange bubble room popped out of existence and he was now standing under a perfectly clear starry night sky. Although puzzled by the child's words he felt almost at peace, at least for a moment until reality set in once more.

Luke realised that he was standing in a ditch up to his ankles in mud, he did not care. He noticed an unusual silence for the night around these parts. No crickets chirped, no wind blew, silence except for the sound of sobbing. Luke directed his gaze to Aaron, expecting to find him as the source of this mournful sound. Aaron lay on his back, staring at his hand and at the space where three fingers should be, but he made no sound. No, the sobbing was coming from the direction of the battlefield. Luke moved slowly over the rise, bravely leaving the safety of the ditch to return to the violent scene.

Chapter 12: Ellana's Warning

Hundreds of bodies were chaotically laid out in front of him and amongst the bodies he saw two lone figures. The first figure appeared to be kneeling down holding onto the other figure. From this distance, the light was too poor to make out who they were. As Luke inched forwards, the images of the battle along with the dread associated with it, came flooding back. He could not face the view of the carnage any longer so he decided that he would at least try and tend to Aaron first, as maybe with Aaron in tow he could face the scene and find out who these mysterious figures were. It was strange, Aaron was normally the strong one, but this time that responsibility seemed to be falling to Luke.

"How does Aaron normally handle these situations?," Luke thought. "Well, he rarely takes anything seriously," he thought annoyingly. "However, it does seem to work for him, maybe I should try it".

"Hey Aaron, don't look so glum. At least you will get a five finger discount now, well two anyway." Luke realised how hurtful what he just said could have been, but Aaron stopped staring at his hand for a moment and slowly but surely a smile began to appear on his face, followed by sniggering before eventually laughing out loud, the sort of laughter that only occurs after a life or death situation.

"And they call me the funny one. Here I am all fingerless

and you pour salt onto the wound," Aaron said jokingly. But then he looked back at his hand again and his expression once again turned to depression. "Look, you might want to leave me here. You know I can't be of any help to you now. I guess... I guess I will go home after all. Only I suppose now I would be more of a burden to 'em now."

"Don't talk like that. You helped me, I'm most likely one of the most useless klutz of a fighter you have no doubt ever seen, but I managed to survive. I doubt losing a few fingers would make you much of a lesser man in a fight."

Aaron smiled once again. "To tell you the truth," Aaron said, "I ain't much of a fighter me self either" He held up his hand as if to prove that point. "Archery was my thing, but I won't be firing any more bows, that is for sure. Not sure what I can do now, but hey, at least we're alive, I guess."

"I will find a use for you, don't you worry," Luke smirked.

"You know, you are beginning to sound a bit too much like me. It's worrying, you should really see a head doctor." Aaron joked.

Aaron started to pick himself up and spoke softly, "Well anyway, there is no point sitting around crying over spilt blood and fingers."

Chapter 12: Ellana's Warning

Luke helped Aaron finish getting to his feet, a simple act he too could barely manage. As Aaron grabbed Luke's shoulder, fresh blood squelched out and dripped down from the wound on his arm. Luke howled out in pain. The balm in the bandages Aaron used seemed to quieten the pain quickly once again.

With Aaron by his side, Luke felt he now had the strength to return to the battlefield. Together they approached the centre, and it became clear the identity of the sobbing man. The man was Geal. Geal was knelt on the blood-drenched earth holding his dead son in his arms. Luke knew Geal was a great warrior and would most likely be highly dangerous in this severe emotional state, yet Luke could not bear to leave him like this. He approached the broken man.

"No, " Aaron warned him.

Luke ignored Aaron's advice and stepped into Geal's field of view. Geal looked up and glanced at Luke for but a second before returning the gaze to his dead son.

Geal spoke in almost a whisper at first. "I don't blame you, Luke. I don't even blame the bandits." His voice then grew louder, it was no longer a whisper. "I only blame myself. This was my fault, MY FAULT, I taught him morals, honour and bravery. It was my teachings that got him killed. He died because of those stupid ideals!" With that last word, he let out a primal roar.

"It's all my fault, it's all my fault," he sobbed repeatedly.

Luke felt compelled to attempt to console him, "You could not have wished for a better son. Think of the legacy he has now left behind. Think of what he has done, he slew Traigon, and because of this the bandits of the north will be no more. You are right, it was your fault. You did teach him honour and bravery, but you should be proud of what you did and what he had become".

Geal looked up once more. "What good is bravery and honour now? Tell me. He's dead. Honour and bravery are no help to the dead. I would take everything back, even suffer Traigon forever if it meant I could see my son alive once more! All his death has brought is more death and suffering, to thousands of people. Leave me to my mourning, Luke." Geal's free hand grasped his broadsword and Luke took the hint.

Luke and Aaron left Geal to his son and headed, not for the trail but towards the bandit camp to replenish the supplies stripped from them.

The gates of the bandit camp were ajar, Aaron pushed them fully open and they both entered. They knew full well that bandits could still be there hiding, yet they had

Chapter 12: Ellana's Warning

no choice. The camp lay barren. In each tent it seemed as though scenes from the bandits lives were frozen in time. Food lay half eaten on tables and various gambling games remained half-played, some with even the stakes still in play. The men left it all there in the rush to join the battle.

Luckily no one appeared to be stirring; they must have either fled, hid or died on the spot as the bodies with arrows in their backs testified.

Luke and Aaron gathered and salvaged what they could from the stricken camp. Those that had managed to flee had removed most of the valuable and useful items, meaning it was slim pickings. They did manage to salvage enough food, chits, as well as a couple other odds and ends for their journey west, however. Supplies gathered they did not hang around. They quickly and quietly left the camp and started down the trail.

The journey took them well over a week, their injuries slowing every aspect of the journey down. Bedding down for the night was the worst part of it, the battle seemed to have effected more than just physically. The images of bloodshed and slaughter haunted them every night. They were only getting a few hours of sleep, which made them both extremely irritable.

"Listen you klutz, if you build the fire there the wind will blow the smoke into our eyes. I do not want to become like

Surface

smoked bacon, thank you," Aaron said sarcastically "Build it downwind from us, there," he pointed, "by that rock". Aaron now performed a lot less of the work himself then he would have previously, in fact prior to the battle he would have done most of the work himself, being more adept at these things. Too injured, perhaps? Feeling sorry for himself more likely, Luke thought. In any case he was beginning to get on Luke's nerves, with his new 'commander' approach.

Luke did his best to understand Aaron's predicament and for the most part he succeeded in not showing his annoyance.

They were down to the very last of their scavenged supplies when they eventually stumbled upon the hatch that led down through subterranean tunnels and steep gorges to reach the town of Archesh. As they stood at the hatch, Luke noticed that the sun seemed to set ever earlier in the day. Living underground he had never encountered seasons before.

When Luke started to climb, he noticed that at last his chest was feeling a lot better, though his arm was still painful from the deep cut. However, Aaron's hand would never fully heal; after all severed fingers rarely grow back. Aaron joined Luke on the hundred foot ladder climb descent. Although awkward for Aaron, his nimbleness seemed to overcome his disability, proving to Luke that

Chapter 12: Ellana's Warning

despite what Aaron may think, he was still highly capable.

Aaron stopped for a moment. He needed to get something off of his chest.

"You know, back in the bandit camp, when Traigon was threatening to kill you?"

"Go on...," Luke said, intrigued.

"I know I seemed I was going to let it happen. I was stalling, trying to hatch a plan, I had something up my sleeve, trust me. Obviously I did not want 'em to kill you"

"Good job Geal was there then," Luke joked as he stepped onto the last ladder.

"Well, even if he was not, I was not going to betray you in revealing the chalice's route, I already done that once in the temple I could not do that to you again, even if it did mean your life. Bit daft really, ain't it?" He resumed climbing, "Well yes... I am not sure if I should thank you or kill you, but I guess you were doing what you thought was best," Luke replied as stepped off the bottom rung.

"Err, if I got the choice, can I have option one, please?", Aaron pleaded as he gingerly descended to meet Luke at the bottom.

Surface

After a short walk through a cave passage, they emerged from the rock face to be greeted by a roaring waterfall. They then tiredly made their way through the gorge until at last they saw the welcome sight of the twinkling lights of Archesh. Before they had even managed to enter the town they were met by someone. It was none other than Ellana, who greeted them heartedly. Ellana certainly seemed to be glad to see them, especially Luke, as evident by the smile she directed at him.

"Come, let's get you on your way," she said, as if trying to get rid of them, which was strange as she clearly seemed fond of Luke.

They were led into the town, passing many simple stone dwellings on route. The town was quiet and the people they did see seemed to be almost oblivious to the new visitors. The townspeople simply carried on with their day-to-day lives, be it scrubbing clothes, shoeing horses, or drawing water from the town's well. They barely even batted an eyelid as they strolled by. Strange, considering that Luke thought it was a xenophobic town. Luke also had expected a fuss to be made over him, as there was at the temple. He was glad there was not, as keeping things quiet was certainly a safer option.

Ellana led the pair out of the other side of the village and across a thankfully solid looking stone bridge that overlooked a deep canyon. The canyon separated the small

Chapter 12: Ellana's Warning

temple on the other side from the rest of the town. Despite the failing light of dusk, they could just make out how deep the canyon was and could see a narrow strip of white snaking its way along the bottom. The white snake was the raging torrent they passed earlier, that was now hundreds, if not thousands, of feet below them, almost silent at this distance.

The path widened on the other side of the gorge before ending at the temple with the two windows. As Luke followed the path he was joined to his left by Ellana and on his right walked Aaron. The three of them marched up to the doors of the temple as one. They pushed the doors open, but as they were about to cross the threshold, Ellana stopped them.

"I am afraid, sorry, what is your name?," Ellana asked Aaron.

"Aaron, me lady," Aaron chirped cheekily.

"I am afraid, Aaron, you will have to wait outside." To this, Aaron performed a quick and just as cheeky bow, seeming not to care that this was another thing he was excluded from.

Ellana then disappeared through a side door, leaving Luke waiting in a rather small entrance porch, beyond which, through a wide open door, was the main hall. The doorway was resplendent. Most of the door frame had been carved into decorative figures that all seemed to tell a story. Luke was not sure, but it appeared to him that one of the scenes depicted the entrance to Luke's home. The entrance was surrounded by many small wooden figurines of people stood outside looking out to the horizon. Luke, however, could not make heads or tails of the rest of it.

Luke peered into the hall beyond and noticed that it was similar in design to the hall in the monk's temple, except this time the multi-tiered arching roof was wooden and the hall was only one-third of the scale. Additionally, in the place of the marble seating of the other hall there were instead wooden benches. The benches were lined up to form neat rows, pews if you will. The altar in the centre that the pews centred on held no relic and was little more than a stone platform. There were some stone carvings on the platform, however most were faded or destroyed. The hall itself was void of life, no one stirred.

Luke waited longer and wondered what welcoming committee he could expect, as he was inside the temple away from the prying eyes of the villagers.

Ellana returned and Luke was led through the small side door that led onto a spiral staircase where he was led up several stories. They emerged from the stairs into the eves of the building. The roof space was rather dusty and dank.

Chapter 12: Ellana's Warning

Boxes, barrels and old pews were piled up against the walls. In the centre of the room stood two men, whispering. One was wearing a chalice monk's robe and the other was not. This other man was also not adorned in any finery. He wore simple peasant clothes, the same as the villagers. It was he who was holding the chalice. Where was the group of people in ceremonial outfits he came to expect?

Luke strained to overhear the men's whispers:

"If there is no other way then," whispered the man in peasant clothes.

The men noticed Luke and Ellana. They turned to face them, breaking their conversation mid-sentence.

"We have said what has needed to be said," the monk replied to the other man. The monk moved swiftly to the exit and rushed past Luke without saying a word.

"You, Luke?," the man asked in a gruff voice.

"Yes," Luke replied.

"Then the chalice is yours... anointed one," he proclaimed, but the look he gave was more of fear than gratitude. He turned and left, leaving Ellana and Luke alone.

Surface

"Have I done something wrong, Ellana?," Luke asked.

"Why do you ask?"

"They look at me with such fear and loathing, I thought I was the saviour of their religion? It is strange, Ellana. Thinking about it I noticed that the monks also seemed not to relish helping me. They appeared as if they were just going through the motions because they had to."

Ellana pulled Luke away from the door, making sure that there were no prying eyes that could see them or ears hear them. However, unknown to them, their efforts had failed as Aaron, despite his injury, had managed to scramble up the cliff behind the temple before silently leaping onto the roof. He recognised Luke and Ellana's voices and put his ear to a small hole between the tiles.

Ellana fixed her gaze directly onto Luke making sure she had his attention and spoke, "they do indeed not relish their task for they fear you and what you represent. Do you blame them after what they have had to endure? They don't trust the children any more, for the children brought disaster; however, they also fear what would happen should they defy the children."

Luke was a little confused. He thought reading the texts that they had been a force for good. "Did the children not try to help you, did they not help you begin to build a new

Chapter 12: Ellana's Warning

world?," Luke found him self asking Ellana.

Ellana continued to stare at Luke and replied,
"if they were indeed so good, why did they allow the slaughter of our people? However, despite this a number our people including myself still want you to return the chalice. Maybe there still is hope. It may free your people as you hope, as well as help ours. I will just say one thing. I urge you caution, Luke. I know not what happened to the people before you."

"People before me?," Luke enquired, wondering if Ellana knew more of these past relic seekers he read about.

"Yes. people before you. As you may know, there have already been many relics retrieved. This chalice that you now hold is the last one. We believe it will complete the jigsaw"

"Jigsaw? Do you know more of these people?," Luke pressed.

"A figure of speech. As I already said, I do not know what happened to those before you, All I know is that they have never been seen again, at least on the surface anyway. I hope it was just that they did not like the surface and decided to stay below. After all, I know your society is a sealed society and getting out again I guess would be difficult."

Surface

Luke suspected people had gone missing from the colony, but had only heard rumours. He certainly, never heard of people coming back after going outside. The Hammerites were good at keeping secrets, so perhaps that was why. He then wondered how she came to know so much but thought it was not wise to press her.

"Thank you for the warning Ellana." Luke said.

Luke was grateful that Ellana did not keep any secrets from him. He presumed she would probably get into a lot of trouble if anyone else knew what she had told him. She had talked so candidly about the "children". Luke could be wrong, but he was thinking there might be some sort of bond forming between them that started when she cared for him on his previous visit. Does she now care for him in another sense ? He certainly liked her. After all, she seemed to be a straightforward and kind hearted woman not to mention attractive.

"It's a pity I have to leave" Luke almost said aloud.

Ellana, flashed Luke a smile before exiting the room, leaving him alone with the chalice. She said she would see him outside to escort him back out of town.

Luke thought about Ellana for a moment longer before

Chapter 12: Ellana's Warning

pushing his new feelings aside, for he had more important things to be concentrating on, such as getting home.

Chapter 13: Past Memories

"Traigon had claimed that the chalice holds powers. I wonder if this is true?," Luke pondered as he stared intently at the true chalice.

He had heard that one of the powers was teleportation. Now was as good a time as any to try and access it. Traigon had held the chalice above his head, so that was what Luke did. He noticed the chalice's weight, but nothing else. Then Luke began to envision his home, as if the image would be enough to compel it, but still nothing happened. Maybe there was some trick to it? But he then thought, no, more likely, the powers of the chalice were just lies. After all, surely the powers it was credited with were impossible.

Luke wondered what he was doing even attempting to use the chalice. He felt foolish. Of course the powers were a lie, he knew this. Luke came from what he liked to think of as an advanced society, advanced despite being quite totalitarian. There was certainly no technology at home that could even come close to performing what the chalice was claimed to do. Was there something more, magic perhaps? A definite 'no' would have been the answer, that was until recently. Now he was not so sure. He had seen quite a few things that he could not explain, not least the

Chapter 13: Past Memories

children themselves, they who appeared to have influenced him and the past of the world so profoundly.

Luke further surmised that maybe the powers, if they were indeed mythical; were a lie propagated by the children as a way to entice people to seek out their relics out. Lie or not though, Luke knew the only way he would get any true answers would be to finish the task and return home once more.

Luke exited the building and as expected he was met by Ellana. Aaron, on the other hand, was nowhere to be seen.

There was a pat on Luke's back, followed by a beaming Aaron. It was as if Aaron had just stepped through from another world as he appeared to have just materialised on that spot behind him.

Luke wondered where he had been, but guessed he had just been off exploring… or stealing.

Ellana led them off across the bridge and back into the simple stone built village. In a complete contrast to last time, the people who had previously paid them no heed gathered around them and then followed them through the village. Luke realised to his horror that he had forgotten to hide the chalice properly, it was clearly visible in his grasp.

Surface

Most of the crowd were merely curious while others seemed to be wary of them. There were a few who were not happy at all with their presence, they stared at the trio with angry eyes.

"So it is true then, this man is to return the relic," someone in the crowd announced. There were audible gasps at this from people at the back of the crowd who had not seen the relic themselves.

"So then, the world is to be rebuilt?," someone else asked sarcastically. This statement made Aaron glance at the chalice nervously. Those simple words seem to have fazed him. This was strange, Luke thought, it was almost as if Aaron thought this could actually happen? Luke, of course, was unaware that Aaron had overheard his conversation with Ellana earlier.

Luke, however, could only smile at the remark. After all, this surface world was a savage and barbaric place. If this relic somehow did change it, then all the better.

The more angry members of the crowd circled in front of them, blocking their path, while others blocked the way back behind them. They were then practically herded into a small square with an old overgrown well as its centrepiece.

"The monks are wrong! The chalice should not be

Chapter 13: Past Memories

returned!" Several men and women shouted this, followed by jeering and curses from those and other members of the crowd. More and more began to hurl abuse and protests in their direction. The waves of anger seemed to spread through the crowd. Then something more physical was hurled. A rotten tomato exploded all down the side of Luke's face. Its smelly pulp dribbled down onto his shoulder, leaving a sticky horrid residue as it went.

"Stop this," Ellana shouted, but obviously to no avail as she too was pelted by rotten vegetation; a rotten cabbage exploded in a shower of green leaves and black rot as it struck her thigh. The next projectile was a jagged stone that flew towards Aaron. Luckily Aaron's quick reflexes avoided injury and instead the stone hit an old man in the crowd, almost knocking him unconscious. Blood streamed out from the open wound. The crowd saw the blood, and despite one of their own throwing the stone, all the anger was directed at the three of them as if it was somehow their fault. Mob mentality was setting in, even those who had been merely curious were now ready to set upon the trio.

Luke held the chalice and tried to calm his thoughts. Maybe the chalice would at least be powerful enough to calm the crowd, maybe that power was true. Luke tried to calm himself by imagining he was back home again. He tried to think what it would be like to lay in his warm bed, once more stare at the pictures and videos of the old world

Surface

as he often did. He tried to remember what it was like having nothing else to worry about other than the next repair roster, or staying clear of the Hammers. Yes, it was a boring life, one he would have done anything to leave, but today he felt that way no longer. Today, above all else he wanted to be home.

Luke looked up from the chalice; the world had fallen away, in a cloud of white and blue. The chalice had worked. He was being transported home.

"Luke, move it, run!" Aaron shouted. Then Luke realised that he had not actually moved an inch, instead Aaron had used a smoke bomb, something Luke did not know he even possessed. Maybe this was the trick up his sleeve he would have used back at the bandit camp. Luke ran as fast as he dared not being able to see, in the direction he thought would lead out of the village, hoping to escape before the smoke cleared. He brushed passed several people, friend or foe he did not know. He knew that he had to keep pushing on through the smoke. He felt something solid, a wall. He followed along the wall to where it led him into an alley.

Now feeling two walls his speed increased until he crashed into several barrels of foul smelling liquid, soaking his boats and splashing him all over. Soon the alley walls left him, and he could feel the grass beneath his feet. The smoke began to clear, and the visibility increased,

Chapter 13: Past Memories

Luke could at least see his own hand in front of him. He could now just about make out the main path out of the village and set off running at full pelt, regardless of how much his various injuries complained. After a few hundred yards he had completely cleared the smoke, so he slowed to a walk. He could run no longer anyway. A heavily panting Aaron had stopped just ahead of him, yet Ellana was nowhere to be seen.

They looked back at the village with relief as they could see that no one was following them. The smoke over the village had cleared enough for them to see that the streets were empty. The elders must have restored order, so hopefully Ellana was safe. Luke was forced to resign himself to the fact that if this was not true, there was nothing he could do for her.

They reached the waterfall and were ready to leave the gorge except for just one thing…

"You smell like a manure wagon that crashed into a fish store whose goods were well past their best. Get in that water!," Aaron demanded. Luke sniffed himself and obeyed.

After an invigorating cold shower under the falls, he then changed his clothes, and they set off again. Their pace was swift or at least as swift as their injuries would allow. They entered the tunnels and once again climbed the ladders

Surface

before exiting back onto the surface. They headed north along the Red Way. It was less than a day's journey before they would reach the entrance to Luke's home, an entrance that stood at the bottom of a steep hill leading up to a mountain.

They soon veered off the paved Red Way onto a lesser used trail that could be best described as a mud track. That track led them across a meadow and into deep woodland.

The path they followed lazily meandered its way from tree to tree. Once or twice they had to retrace their steps as parts of the path were hard to follow, being severely overgrown; it was hard going. Despite this, the forest was actually quite a pleasant and peaceful place. Aromas of acorn and tree resin filled their nostrils, birds sang while dancing from branch to branch.

The golden yellow and green canopy grew thicker as they progressed and gradually the forest grew darker, yet many small shafts of light still made their way through. The onset of autumn had made room.

At an old post hole the path split into two. The right hand path seemed to all but disappear as ferns and bushes covered it almost entirely, leaving a particularly narrow gap to indicate there was once a trail. The way on looked more likely to be the left hand path where there was evidence that people had used this path more recently,

Chapter 13: Past Memories

such as an old dried mud patch where faded foot prints and cart tracks could be found. Luke surmised that one of these tracks probably belonged to Ellana, made all those many weeks ago, when she dragged his unconscious body through the forest. Luke could only imagine the difficulty Ellana had when dragging him through this terrain. Ellana had certainly gone out of her way to help a complete stranger.

Luke strangely felt compelled to take the right fork despite it not being the right way, his dangerous curiosity was getting a better of him again. The last time it did that it caused him to end up in this dangerous world. As he started along the path it quickly became apparent that he would not get far when the foliage grew denser. Unperturbed he pushed his way through until he emerged into a small clearing. At the end of the clearing was a large free-standing stone. It looked man made. Aaron, who had followed, seemed to be nervous. He knew what sort of people and creatures ruins often attracted. He advised Luke that they should turn back. However, Luke ignored this advice and decided to investigate further. The stone looked as if it had once been inscribed, but it was now completely unreadable. From where he was stood now Luke could see more buildings beyond the clearing, so he hacked his way through the undergrowth on the other side to get a better look.

Luke expected to find just some old husk of an old country

Surface

lodge or farmhouse. Indeed that did appear to be the case. However, there was not just one husk, there were many, spread out amongst the trees. Most of which were nothing more than outlines. This gave the area the appearance of blueprints for a settlement that is still yet to be built.

As he started to wander deeper, the forest grew less dense, and he could see yet more and more ruins. He now knew that the ruins that he first saw were in fact only a small part of a large complex of buildings, a town most likely, at least what was left of one. The forest seemed to have reclaimed most of it. The ruins must have been at least a hundred years old as mature oak trees grew from within them. One building caught his attention. He noticed that unlike the others, this building was not constructed from simple stone, wood or brick; it was constructed from concrete, like many of the interior walls of his old home. Unlike his home, however, these walls crumbled to the touch.

Between the concrete, metal rebarb poles jutted up at regular intervals. This pattern was repeated on more and more buildings as Luke delved deeper still into the ruins. It looked as if he was staring into a field of wheat, only the wheat was metal rebarb. Maybe the ruins were from before the time of ice Luke thought, but then he doubted that as he was sure nothing would exist from those times as ice and water would have wiped out or buried all traces. No these ruins had to be more recent than that.

Chapter 13: Past Memories

Luke carefully stepped over the various walls and undergrowth and entered the central clearing, passing under the remains of an archway as he did so. In the centre there were no more structures, nor trees or grass, just bare earth on which nothing grew. Stood in the centre was one simple stone, a stone that bore a many worded inscription. Luke stepped forward and began to read. It was strangely in his language…

"Be mindful of trust, be mindful of ignorance, lest you join the fallen," it read. Below that was text of a much smaller size, so small after over a hundred or so years of decay it was now barely visible. Luke ,however, could read enough to know that this was a list of names, hundreds of names: men, women and children. The list continued around to the back of the stone, a list of the dead he surmised.

"Yeovin," Aaron quietly said behind a now slightly startled Luke, as if that one word would explain all.

"Yeovin?," Luke repeated.

"This was one of the first founder towns. I am told it was a prosperous town until just like all the founder towns one night everyone just disappeared. No one knows why and no one knows where to. We can only presume they died from whoever put this plaque here".

Surface

"I know what happened" Luke said simply in a depressed tone under his breath. He knew what part in history this place had played. Aaron's people, Luke surmised, were too ashamed to record the truth, so that is why Aaron, and likely anyone else, did not know the true version of events. This town's place in history and others like it had been eradicated from history just like the people who once lived within. The pilgrims, his people who were so wrongly slaughtered a hundred years ago should not be forgotten. He would tell Aaron the truth, he would tell everyone the truth, but now was not the time.

Luke did not want to leave this place, he wanted to learn as much about it as he could. Aaron, on the other hand, wanted to leave immediately. He was restless and edgy. When Aaron was not jumping at shadows, his eyes were darting from side-to-side, watching for danger. Luke did not find anything more. It appears that the ruins had been looted long ago. The forest grew darker as twilight was setting in, and it was at this point when Aaron finally persuaded Luke to leave, as Luke came to realise he would find nothing more. Together they swiftly returned to the main trail before the light faded altogether.

They tried to light their torches, but they refused to ignite; the air was just too humid. In this deep darkness, the forest's character changed significantly. What had previously only been curiously shaped tree branches now looked like twisted arms ready to reach out and grab them

Chapter 13: Past Memories

and pull them into the darkness. Cracks and rustles in the underbrush became more pronounced. It sounded to them like a pack of large feral animals were tracking them and at any moment they would pounce. It was, therefore a moment of great relief when the trees parted and they emerged into open heathland under a clear night sky. There was no longer any need for torches the strong moonlight lit the way for them.

To their left was the old stone wall, Luke saw when he started this journey. This was the wall where his equipment was stripped from him and also the last time he saw any of his people. Up the hill at the end of the wall, as if highlighted by the moon, were the large blast doors shielding Luke's old home from the outside world.

Luke found himself running. He quickly left Aaron behind as he shot uphill towards the doors, hoping they would just open up and let him in. The doors, however, remained closed, so Luke was forced to bound to a stop. Breathlessly Luke began inspecting the thick concrete walls surrounding the doors, desperately hoping to find some sort of switch or intercom, but there was nothing. By now Aaron had eventually caught up. He persuaded Luke that it would be better for them to get some rest and bed down for the night. They would have better luck in the morning.

They unrolled their canvas coverings and began setting up their camp. 'Clunk'. They both stopped what they were doing. The sound was followed by a loud high-pitched whirring noise that emanated from the sealed entrance. Motors sprung to life. A yellow beam of light shot out from under the metal doors, illuminating them and the surrounding area as the door began to rise. They had to look away for a moment, the light was so bright to their dark adjusted eyes. Blinking into the light they could see that a concrete hallway had been revealed. Strangely, there was no one there to greet them, Luke did not know if this was a good thing or not.

They entered through the yawning doorway and stepped into the airlock. As they stood there, Luke did not know which one of them was more nervous. The heavy door behind them reversed and slid slowly down behind them before coming to a rest with a large metal crash. The bright artificial yellow light above went out.

For a moment, Aaron thought he was trapped. There was a whoosh of strange smelling air before the door in front began to creep and rattle upwards. The door banged loudly several times as caught momently on its sliders. Each bang made Aaron jump backwards a little bit until finally his back was pressed up against the outer door.

This door revealed no one either, "Why would there be, this place is forbidden after all", Luke thought.

Luke did not notice last time that the floor was covered in

Chapter 13: Past Memories

at least a good few centuries worth of dust. There were several sets of foot prints. One he knew was his, and his silent Hammerite guards, but there were many others that he could not account for, some more recent than others, as measured in the thickness of the dust that had resettled.

"You lived here?," Aaron asked in puzzlement.

Luke practically ignored the question, he only managed a quick nod of his head. He was too engrossed in examining the passageway as he did not have the chance to last time when he was marched outside.

Another thing that Luke did not notice last time was that part of the left hand wall had been plastered in crumbling paint. He could see the faded outlines of a yellow rectangle containing faded black lettering. Despite the degradation Luke could read the text. It said "Bunker 54". Interesting, but meaningless. Luke continued to examine the rest of the passageway. He noticed remains of what appeared to have been chairs that once lined a section of wall. Now only the rusty metalwork and mouldy scraps of fabric remained. This corridor was once some sort of waiting room, Luke surmised.

Moving down the corridor he could see faded scraps of old paper and broken glass scattered around in another corner. He stooped to pick up one of the pieces of paper, but it completely disintegrated in his hand. Luke imagined the founders of his people must have walked through here many millennia ago. They must have read those old papers, and sat in those chairs.

Luke moved on and passed under the air shaft, he had passed months before. Aaron then followed. They rounded a corner before reaching the end of the passage where a vacant lift carriage awaited them, ready to take them down.

"You don't have to come, you know," Luke said quietly to Aaron.

"I have nothing better to do, I may as well get into trouble somewhere new. After all, it has been… fun so far," Aaron joked.

Aaron's motivations remained a mystery. Luke could tell that Aaron was nervous and guessed he was only coming along due to some sort of perceived loyalty. Perhaps it was to make up for his earlier betrayal when he attempted to steal the chalice from him? Or perhaps in his injured state he had nowhere else to go? So had their roles now been reversed? Did Aaron now depend on Luke? After all, what use is there for a thief with seven digits?

They both stared at the blank walls beyond the lift's opening. Neither of them knew what to expect and how they would be treated. Aaron, a total stranger, a complete

Chapter 13: Past Memories

outsider, and Luke, well, he had been banished never to return. Many most likely thought of him as dead.

They stepped into the lift and that now familiar puzzled look appeared on Aaron's face. What is the point of this room?, his face seemed to say. Aaron was about to ask Luke why they were standing in this box, but he was cut short as the doors closed behind them and the lift jolted to a start. Slowly they began to move downwards. Luke could have sworn he heard Aaron yelp as they began to accelerate faster and faster. Through the gaps in the doors they could see lights lining the shaft flying past them, casting shadows for an instant on the back wall of the lift. Faster still they went, the lift was travelling much faster than it did on its upwards journey previously. Fifty miles per hour.. sixty... Was the lift out of control? Were they about to become a mashed pulp at the bottom of the shaft, so that the Hammerites could claim the chalice from their mangled corpses? Ten seconds passed, the lights were now becoming a blur, twenty seconds.

The floor of the lift began to vibrate and shudder and the lift began slowing rapidly. The brakes had come on causing sparks to fly as the metal grinded. The lift stopped. The force of the sudden de-acceleration slammed both of them to the floor. Slowly they got to their feet from their embarrassing positions on the lift floor and dusted themselves off. They stared forwards, awaiting the opening of the doors.

Chapter 14: Home Life

Luke and Aaron did not have to wait long for the lift doors to slide open, and before Luke could even exit the lift he was suddenly ambushed. Antheria gripped him in a vice like, but warm embrace. She would not let go. To his surprise she kissed him too, fully on the lips.

Luke had no idea she felt this way about him. They were good friends, true, but this seemed much more than merely welcoming home a good friend. True, he had once wished to move things further, but had never actually been brave enough to take the first step. He had resigned himself to just being friends. He wished he had known that actually, she wanted the same thing.

Now, however, he was richer in experience. After all, he had survived the many perils of the outside world. Surely now he had within him the courage to take that next step. Had Antheria already taken that step with that welcoming embrace? These were thoughts that swirled around in Luke's head. He vowed to himself that once the chalice business was concluded he would take that step.

Eventually, Antheria released her grip and Luke was finally able to see beyond her. A crowd had gathered on a platform connecting to a walkway leading outwards.

Chapter 14: Home Life

Antheria gently gripped Luke's left hand and slowly led him from the lift to be surrounded by the crowd. Aaron was reluctant to join them, and for now at least he remained inside the lift out of sight.

The crowd was silent, no murmurs or talking could be heard. From the silence came the sound of a single person clapping, before more joined in until soon the whole crowd burst out into a full-blown applause.

"The anointed one has returned with the relic!", they cheered and yelled.

Luke looked at their admiring faces. Some he thought he recognised from a time long ago, but most he had never seen before in his life. He knew that these people were Hammerites as they wore the familiar grey uniform with a golden hammer emblazoned on the chest. Yet strangely against the norm, they wore no masks. Luke's gaze moved away from the admiring crowd as he could not help but to be drawn in by his magnificent surroundings, a place he never knew existed.

The lift and the platform were the centrepiece of a completely spherical chamber that must have measured more than two hundred feet in diameter and in height. The platform he was stood on surrounded the shaft and was suspended, attached to the lift shaft one hundred feet off of the floor. Noticeably the floor and ceiling were adorned at regular intervals with giant golden hammers that were not decoration; they were a source of light, they glowed like hot branding irons.

Stretching away from the lift and platform was a walkway that led to the edge of the chamber. On the connecting far wall stood some large double doors, made from metals of various colours. The doors appeared to be the only other visible exit from the chamber. To the side of the doors was another walkway. This walkway skirted all the way around the edge of the chamber as it spiralled its way down to the chamber floor. The floor of the chamber was flat, not spherical. It was as if the bottom of the sphere had been filled with a liquid metal that had since cooled and hardened to form a flat surface. In the centre of this surface stood a large metal table, maybe another altar? Sat atop this "altar," if that was indeed a correct description, were many interesting and strange objects. Each object was housed in its own plastic cylinder so that they did not touch.

Luke was too high up to know for sure what these objects were, but he could safely bet that these were the other relics he had heard about. He noticed that one cylinder was empty, most likely it was reserved for the chalice.

Luke was gripped by the arm, this interrupted his gaze. His free hand was held in the air while another man took the chalice from his backpack and held it above his head.

Chapter 14: Home Life

"Three cheers for the anointed one" the crowd roared.

"Hooray!" "Hooray!..." There was no third cheer; instead the crowd grew ominously silent. Their eyes turned and they all looked in one direction. Luke followed their eyes to where they met Aaron, who had stepped out from his hiding place within the lift.

"Who is this, man?" Luke recognised the owner of the voice. It was that same sombre voice of the judge who had sentenced him to be banished. Luke had hoped he would not be here, for he despised the man.

The man stepped forward from the crowd, his long flowing silver hair fluttered with every one of his trademark long strides. He was a tall man and towered over both Luke and Aaron by almost a complete foot. His pointed nose seemed to complement the menacing presence that his height alone gave him. Luke wondered how he did not notice him in the crowd until now. Too preoccupied he thought, was the most likely reason.

"This is...," Luke said too quietly before increasing the volume of his voice.

"This is Aaron, a man who saved my life on more than one occasion."

Surface

At this, Aaron smiled and then performed his usual cheeky bow.

"Really? Him? If so, that is good to hear." The judge paused "Nevertheless he is still an outsider and as so he cannot be trusted. Take him away!," he demanded.

The silver haired judge turned to Luke and spoke in a softer voice.

"Do not fret, Luke. If what you say is true then he will come to no harm. We just need to be sure he means us no harm. However, I regret to say that our laws forbid him to stay. He will have to leave, after the interview."

Luke did not like the sound of this "interview". He wondered what would happen to Aaron and where he would go afterwards if he was not allowed stay. Perhaps, back to his family?, Luke wondered.

"You promise he will not be harmed? Is there any way I can make you change your mind about letting him stay? Could you not bend the rules in this case?," Luke inquired. But he knew full well that he was not truly in the position to bargain.

"I promise no harm, but as I said the law binds my hands on an outsider's presence," the judge said to both of them as Aaron was grabbed around his shoulders and dragged

Chapter 14: Home Life

away.

"Now regarding you, Luke."

The judge produced what looked to be a well used and certainly ancient looking ceremonial parchment. Yet the golden gilded rolls still glistened in the light as he unfurled it. The judge cleared his throat, ready to speak the words written on the parchment.

"I, Senior Fredrick Olsworth of the Hammers and judge of the people, do hereby bestow the rank of Apostle of the Hammers on this person: Luke Foster, and furthermore absolve him of any and all past crimes. This is recognition of Luke Foster's work in successfully acquiring and returning a relic and in the hope that he will serve us further still." Fredrick put the parchment away and spoke the following official line ,unscripted, "I request that Luke Foster as part of his new duties attends the relic joining ceremony tomorrow on the day of Friday, September 13th 13,604." He paused, directing his gaze at Luke, "Do you accept your duties and the invitation, Luke?"

It was another one of those questions with only one answer, like the one the monks had asked him before he set off with the relic. He replied now as he did then. Turning down the Hammerites would likely not end pleasantly.

Surface

"I accept the duties and invitation," Luke said officially with well hidden reluctance. Fredrick smiled, so did Luke because he had the realisation that finally he would be rid of the relic and the children. Maybe now his life could go back to normal, better than normal in fact. He gazed at Antheria.

"May I return home while I await the ceremony" Luke asked.

"Well..." Fredrick said, "It is irregular."

"Let the man have some rest," someone in the crowd shouted.

Fredrick smiled again with only a small hint of malice. "So be it," he sighed. Reluctant though he was, Fredrick was certainly being kinder to Luke when compared with their last meeting.

"Your robe and mask will be delivered to your abode. Be here and fully robed at 9am sharp," he barked. A wave of nausea hit Luke as it suddenly dawned on him what he had agreed to. He would become a Hammer now, and so he would not be able to return to his old life after all. Hammerites did not mix with everyone else except on official business.

A thought occurred to Luke that quickly calmed him

Chapter 14: Home Life

again, "as they see me as this hero relic seeker I may be able to use this to my advantage and ask for a further favour. I will ask if I will be allowed to return to my old life." This thought bounced about his head, but it did not fully dismiss the rising sickness from his belly.

The gathered people all began to make their way along the walkway. Someone patted Luke on the back before whispering in his ear, "Do not worry my friend, it will be okay. I was once like you. Know that this is a good life, my friend," as if sensing Luke's concern.

"Like me?," Luke asked as he turned around to see who had spoken. Luke did not know this person, but he could see that there was kindness in this ageing man's eyes.

"Yes, like you. You see I was the one who returned that sceptre down there." He pointed down to the bottom of the chamber before clasping his hands together with pride as if grabbing a trophy.

This was a revelation. So this is what happened to the relic seekers before him. They became Hammerites, at least one of them did anyway.

"I should not say more, but feel free to speak to me sometime after you are made a full member and I will tell you all about it. This lot you see are fed up with my old stories". The man shook his head. "Excuse me." He then

Surface

stepped back and rejoined the group.

The crowd with Luke at the rear headed for the only exit of the chamber, all except for Fredrick that is, who had instead begun to descend the spiral of walkways to the floor, no doubt to set the chalice in its rightful place.

The group approached the large metal doors, which opened of their own accord to reveal a large wide stone staircase that stretched upwards far into the distance. The stairs appeared to be carved from the very rock itself, though they were polished to a sheen by years of traffic.

They left the chamber behind and began to ascend.

The ascent continued for a long time, step after step. Luke's weary legs complained more and more. It was not just his legs complaining. "Why must we take the stairs and not the lift?," one of the crowd wheezed as sweat dripped off him.

"Well, how else are we meant to keep fit to stop those runners?", another one joked.

"Well, maybe if there was a reason and you told them that reason you would not have to chase them," Antheria blurted seriously while staring at Luke.

She, like Luke had always been a rebel when it came to the

Chapter 14: Home Life

Hammerites and their policies. Antheria did have a good point. People would likely not run if they knew the truth. Luke would not have if he had been told about this slaughter of his people, except maybe to get revenge. Luke was surprised that she seemed to have got away with her remark. He knew from her clothes that she had not been made a Hammer, so even simple implied remarks could be highly dangerous indeed. Luke further realised that she was in fact very lucky to even be allowed here, in this most forbidden place. How did she come to be here?, Luke wondered.

The two men in the conversation she interrupted merely stared at Antheria, not saying a word. Shortly afterwards, ignoring her entirely, they returned to complaining about the stairs as if nothing had been said.

"What's was that about?," Luke whispered to Antheria.

"Tell you later," Antheria whispered back.

Eventually, after passing several landings, they reached the top of the stairs. All the landings they passed had no exits, all but the last one, which had an innocuous dull grey painted wooden door in one of the walls. Luke thought it was best not to inquire where this led.

They reached the end of the stairs and another set of double doors barred their way. These doors seemed to stick and would not open. One of the crowd members opened a hidden access panel to the side and began tapping away at a keypad inside in what appeared to be a vain effort to try and open the doors. However, all the man got for his efforts was frustration and beeps from the complaining panel. Another man tried and was successful. The doors clicked and opened slightly, but slammed shut again to the groans of several people in the crowd.

"Bloody things, I wish they would allow maintenance down here to look at this door. Twice now it has done this."

The doors clicked open again, "Well I can…" Luke began to say, but before he could finish his sentence another person booted the doors wide open from the force of the blow. The crowd cheered and began to filter out.

They stepped from the stairs into a vast courtroom. This was the room where Luke had faced his trial. The people around suddenly became more sombre. They all swiftly reached within their robes and pulled out their black and white masks. Now in their full attire the crowd split up and disbursed through various exits without saying a word.

Luke was alone in the vast court. He noticed that he was feeling rather faint, he had after all not had much if any sleep in some time But it was also because he was

Chapter 14: Home Life

standing in the place where this all started.

Luke then noticed something out of the corner of his eye. There was someone or something in the upper stands. Was it a child? Luke tried to get a better look, but as he directed his weary eyes directly towards the shape, the shape vanished. His eyes darted around trying to locate the missing shape, but there was nothing there. Was he being paranoid?

Noticing now that everyone was leaving or had already left, Luke called out for Antheria, but she had already made her way out of the courtroom too.

Luke exited up the main staircase that led up and out of the amphitheatre shaped courtroom. He then passed through the glass entrance doors and out into the large void in the rock that he once and would again call home. He strode out across the rocky floor of the enormous central chamber towards a relatively small structure on the other side. It was strangely quiet, which made Luke remain feeling uneasy. The patterns of shadows from the walkways above made the chamber seem like a huge spider web. This did not help to ease his anxiety. He was not sure why he still felt uneasy, he should not as he was finally home. He reached the small building on the other side. To say the building was small was a bit misleading, It stood five stories high and was thirty meters across; it was just dwarfed by everything else in this massive chamber.

Surface

He entered the building and headed up a flight of stairs and exited at the second floor. He then walked down then a corridor and stopped at the room numbered Two-Zero-Eight. He entered the code One-Seven-Four-Two on the keypad next to the door. The door clicked as it mechanically unlocked itself and Luke pushed it open.

His small but welcoming two room apartment was just as he had left it. His robotic fish still swam happily in the large aquarium on the right. His personal effects and work clothes still lay on his bed. The backpack he normally took when he went off 'exploring' still lay propped up against his bedroom cabinet. The pictures of the outside world from ancient times still hung above his bed. The shower... he certainly missed having warm showers.

He had not yet managed to thoroughly remove the horrible and foul smell produced by the substance he stepped in back at the village. He dropped all his clothes and dived right into the shower.

After the shower Luke sat down on his bed, partially clothed.

For the first time since back at the temple in what seemed like months ago, Luke felt that he could relax. He fell asleep for a short while but soon awoke again with thoughts swimming around in his head. He could not help

Chapter 14: Home Life

but to feel sorry about what had happened to Aaron. He tried to console himself by saying he was sure he would come to no harm. Tomorrow after the ceremony he could see about trying to get him released.

He sat up again, staring at his fish as he would have often done after a particularly hard day. He found that watching them swim calmed his mind and made him forget his woes. He tried to imagine himself sitting by the side of a lazy brook, casting a line into the stream under a crisp autumn sky, not caring if he caught anything or not. However, even this day dreaming was difficult as now he knew what the outside world was actually like. He wished he could go back to those days before. At least when he thought the world was naught but ice, he would dream that one day it would melt. Finally though he drifted off to sleep.

His rest was short-lived as there was a knock at his door. He ignored it at first, thinking it was just one of the Hammers delivering his robes. They can come back later, he thought as the ceremony was not for at least another twelve hours. After a pause there was another knock.

"Well, I suppose I better get up," he said aloud with a loud sigh. He slipped on some fresh clothes and got ready to greet the Hammerite, who was probably rather irate by now at being kept waiting.

Surface

More, louder knocking at the door. Luke was being deliberately slow.

"Hello? Luke? Are you there?," someone with a female voice shouted. Luke instantly recognised who it was, it was Antheria.

In a burst of speed Luke bolted to the door release control, while at the same time pulling his shirt down over his head, almost tumbling over a footstool in the process. He pressed the control and the door slid silently open.

"Hello again, Luke,' she said with an almost coy smile. "Sorry I disappeared so quickly earlier, I was halfway to my home before I realised you were not behind me."

Luke only mustered a smile in response.

"Do you want to come in?," Luke found himself asking eventually.

Antheria nodded. She walked past him and sat in Luke's comfy red chair. Luke chose to stay standing rather than to sit down as his bed was the only other place that was available. This visit was nothing unusual, they often visited each other's places and enjoyed a few drinks before wandering off around the complexes, or heading to the one and only bar. So having Antheria over was nothing new, but he could feel that things this time were different,

Chapter 14: Home Life

and clearly more awkward. Luke noticed that Antheria could not seem to stop fidgeting with her hair.

"Listen, Luke..." Antheria began, before stopping as if she could not get the words to surface. "Luke...," she began again, "I have been thinking. Now that you are back, I am wondering if you would like to get me that drink you promised me before you left. I mean you surely owe me a drink if not two by now!," she said with a broad smile.

The only place you could get an alcoholic drink in Luke's world was a place people came to know as "The Broken Shaft". It was originally a simply recreation room, but over time became converted into a bar, supplied by barley grown in a secret farm, in a hidden away chamber. The only reason the Hammerites had not shut it down was because they too enjoyed a tipple now and again, that and the bribes they received.

Luke did not have to be a genius to figure out that Antheria was only using the drink he owed her as an excuse, she definitely had something to say to him. Luke was starting to think that maybe this meeting meant something more than just a couple of friends getting together, a date perhaps?

"I don't know, when it comes to credits and drinks, you never forget do you?," Luke joked before adding, "Go on then," with a big grin on his face too. Luke reached down

Surface

to grab his socks and shoes, but he paused inches off his second shoe.

"Are we allowed, should we... should I even be out in public? After all, am I not suppose to be dead, executed?," he asked.

"Nonsense" she said and added, "Since when have you cared about rules anyway?." She laughed, "Besides, a few days after you were taken I heard that there had been an announcement. People were told that there had been a last minute reprieve and you had been spared death as you had agreed to help the Hammerites"

"I what!", Luke shouted.

"Don't worry, I knew that was not true, but you are now helping them now, are you not?," she asked whilst slightly startled by the outburst.

Luke could not believe it. This was true. He was indeed helping them. He never thought that he would see this day, and he could not help but to feel guilty as he soon would be turning his back on his principles in helping those that had oppressed him and his friends.

Luke eventually shrugged in response to the question. "With that revelation, now I definitely need a drink, lets go."

Chapter 14: Home Life

Luke finished putting his socks and shoes on and they made their way to the top floor of Luke's building and entered the "The Broken Shaft". It was an uncomplicated bar, nothing special, except it gave a nice view of the main chamber. "The Broken Shaft" was a place where Luke would spend too much of his free time watching people come and go. It was the people who were staring at him this time, however. Their faces seemed to say, how could you?

The pair found a quiet table in the corner. Luke bought that drink he owed her and they began talking about old times. They laughed and joked about the various scrapes they both had gotten themselves into over the years. By the time they exhausted this subject, Luke had by now bought Antheria not one but three drinks, and he was just about to buy the fourth. Antheria claimed that Luke owed her a drink for each week he was missing. It had been just over six weeks.

"Only that long?," Luke said.

Luke was glad he had not been away for several months as if he had he soon would be extremely poor, not to mention passed out under the table.

The laughing and joking continued...

Surface

"So you got that old coot to cover for you when you covered for me? Very good. That was the first time I left for the upper levels wasn't it? That was for three days! Antheria, how you got him to do it, I do not know, but you amaze me!" They laughed some more.

They were both remained silent for a moment as each of them tried to think of something else to say.

"I went looking for you, Luke, when you left,' Antheria said quietly.

"Hmm?," was all that Luke could muster in response. He was too busy gazing at Antheria and so had failed to take in what she had just said. He was practically daydreaming, and he could not be happier.

"I ventured out, out to the outside world." She pointed upwards, "I know the truth".

These statements certainly made Antheria regain Luke's attention. She had been outside to that savage world too?

"You should not have, that is a dangerous place," Luke scolded her, his euphoric mood ending.

"I went looking for you!," Antheria repeated loudly which temporally stopped Luke entering into a rant about her safety.

Chapter 14: Home Life

They paused again, staring at each other. At the end of the pause Luke spoke as a smile returned to his face. "I am grateful that you cared so much for me, but you could have been hurt, caught or even killed. What were you thinking?" Luke was surprised with himself. He realised how much of a hypocrite he was being and wished immediately that he could take back what he had just said.

Antheria, however, nodded in agreement.

"It was stupid, I know that now. I was almost killed. Worse, I was caught. I was apprehended almost straightaway. I barely had time to take in the amazing sky before being rushed back underground. Restrained, I thought I was done for. I thought I would be executed, except… except the person who caught me, was Jason. As you know I have known him for years and come to know him as a friend, yet in all that time I never suspected he was a Hammerite. He was always kind to me and others so frankly he did not seem like the sort. He even helped you out once did he not? Perhaps we do judge them too harshly."

Luke stared at her blankly. He thought about what she said about the Hammerites. "Judge them too harshly? Has she forgotten what they have done to hundreds of people? But then who knows what is true any more?," he thought

Surface

silently.

"So anyway...", Antheria said, snapping Luke out of it, "When he caught me I could see how conflicted he was. I convinced him that he could not let them execute me. So instead he smuggled me back in unseen through another entrance atop the mountain, one day's hike away. He told me only a select few people know about the entrance even amongst the Hammerites. This was fortunate for him as he would have most likely been executed on the spot before he had time to explain if caught smuggling someone back in. Such a kind man to risk his life like that."

Luke's face dropped. He was glad Jason kept her safe, but he could not help but to feel jealous of this man, a man whose good looks and suave style was enough to make him sick. What is more, Antheria certainly liked Jason. How much, he did not know. Luke did not like where the conversation was going. Was she about to say she was in a relationship with Jason and this outing was a way of letting him down? Or was what happened just another case of Antheria using her charms to her advantage again?

Antheria noticed the worried look that had developed on top of the saddened features on Luke's face

"I know what you are thinking, and partly you are right, Jason does want there to be more between us. But I have

Chapter 14: Home Life

been holding out because I know that the world out there is not…," her voice shrank to a whisper so that no one would overhear ,"…is not an icy wasteland and so I knew, I hoped, that one day you would return and today you did."

Antheria drew breath, "So I cannot wait any longer, I must know, do you have feelings for me? Feelings other than that of the bonds of friendship?," she enquired and hoped.

Luke did not answer immediately because, in truth he was not sure of the answer. It was all so quick and sudden. He had always considered Antheria a friend. He had always felt warmness to her, but it was not until this very day, after those many weeks apart did those feelings begin to grow. Was it too early to tell?

Antheria began to fiddle with her hair, a trait that Luke knew meant she was getting anxious. Luke, however, still did not answer. The more Luke thought about it the more he realised what the answer should be, so he answered.

"I do, I mean I really do like you" he replied, knowing that the only way to tell for sure was to explore these feelings further and take things further.

He did not go as far as saying he loved Antheria, but what he said was enough and sincere. She immediately leaned across the table, knocking over their drinks in the process.

Surface

She once again embraced him in her bear hug grip, kissing him even more passionately than she did before. He ensured that she too felt the pressure of the embrace and returned this kiss whole-heartedly.

Shortly they noticed everyone was staring at them, so they slowly released their embrace and slid back into their chairs. Luke felt wet, his chest was covered in his drink and it was now dribbling down onto his leg. He hoped Antheria would get the next round to replace this one.

"Luke, I am going to have to go on shift soon, and I am sure you will need to get some rest before the ceremony tomorrow." Luke once again gazed at Antheria. He had to stop himself from saying that maybe she should not go on shift and instead they should continue this elsewhere, maybe go back to Luke's. However, at the last second Luke decided against his characteristic directness. Just as well as it was probably a bad idea at this early stage of the none too certain relationship. They would have all the time in the world to explore things slowly in days, weeks and months to come after the ceremony.

Antheria beamed a smile that sent Luke's head swimming before saying goodbye for now, and thus left him with the mess of spilt drinks upon the table.

Chapter 15: Full Circle

Despite how tired he was, Luke still had trouble getting to sleep that night and when he finally did his dreams were troubling and vivid. There was one dream in particular, a dream where he was holding on for his life as he hung onto something with just one hand. Below him was a seemingly bottomless abyss. For some reason his grip failed, and he fell. As he fell he actually felt the wind rush past him at greater and greater speeds. Then he was enveloped in darkness, he was surrounded by nothing, he was nothing. He thought he was dead, he was alone and screaming in a dark void only for no one to hear. After an agonizing time the dream eventually ended and Luke awoke in a sweat with his voice hoarse.

He gathered his thoughts and swiftly got out of bed before he fell asleep again. It was then he noticed that someone had been in his room. A robe and mask were laid out neatly on the rug at the foot of his bed, ready for him to wear. This was a reminder, if he ever needed one, that there was no true privacy in this place.

After a quick breakfast, he reluctantly donned the cloak and mask and silently left his room so as not to disturb his neighbours. He did not want them to see who he had or at least soon would become. He sighed. He probably would have to move out after this was done and move into the

Surface

Hammer accommodation in the higher levels. His thoughts then turned to Antheria. He hoped that his new status would not make an impossible barrier between them, perhaps Antheria could join too?

He made his way back across the great central chamber, through the courtroom and down the seemingly never-ending stairs. With his knees decidedly tender, he finally reached the bottom and entered the relic chamber, as he now decided to call it.

Everyone was already assembled. They were all sat waiting for him on simple wooden stools; funny, he did not think he was late. Luke was glad that someone else had carried all those chairs down all those stairs and even happier that he would not be the one taking them back up again, unless for some strange reason that was what the ceremony entailed. Luke spotted and then sat on the only unoccupied stool. It creaked and wobbled as he slowly lowered his weight onto it. No doubt this was why it was the last remaining stool.

The sounds the stool made drew in many nearby eyes, including Fredrick's. He looked visibly irritated. Fredrick wasted no time and quickly cleared his throat for another speech, one that Luke hoped would be short.

"Long have we waited for the last relic, and now it is finally in our midst. The man responsible is sat here" He

Chapter 15: Full Circle

pointed, "This man is Luke!" The crowd applauded and cheered and began a mantra: "Luke! Luke! Luke!" Luke blushed.

Fredrick held up both of his hands and the crowd quietened again.

"Today, as the children once predicted, we will now combine the relics and move onto the final phase of the children's plan, a plan that will be of benefit to us all". Luke did hope that Fredrick would elaborate on what this mysterious plan was, but instead he uncharacteristically kept his speech short and simple. He stepped over to the altar and began to remove each relic from its cylindrical container in turn and placed each neatly onto a raised section of the altar. First he placed the hammer, then the ornate rod, the golden plate was next and then what looked like a simple metal spike. Finally, he placed the sceptre before resting the hammer on top of them all. He uttered no ceremonious words;,instead he just stood back and waited.

Nothing happened... at first.

Luke could not be sure, but it appeared as if the objects were starting to shimmer, not only shimmering but also they seemed to be becoming translucent as if turning to glass. Fredrick slowly stepped further back from the altar, just in time too because as he did so, huge shafts of lightning began to arc from the protruding, features of the relics. The lightning struck the hammer symbols that adorned the room with almighty crashes; the room appeared to be the centre of a massive electrical storm. Luke's hair by this time was standing to attention. When Luke was not blinded by the bright flashes he could see that the relics were now entirely transparent, their shapes had become indistinct as they merged into a singular swirling mass.

The room grew brighter still as the arcs of lightning grew more violent; many arcs were now striking simultaneously. Then there was one final bright white flash. With that the room dimmed again, the violent transmogrification had come to an end. Luke's vision took a while to adjust to the comparatively dim light. The glowing hammer symbols on the walls diminished until the only light they provided was that of a previous night's camp fire. In front of him, in place of the relics, stood a perfect sphere that was barely six inches in diameter. But the sphere was not the only new thing in the room. Arranged in a semicircle around the altar stood thirteen ghostly children. The middle child stepped forward; he looked older than the rest, perhaps thirteen or fourteen years of age. Perhaps he was the leader, Luke thought, the rest looked to be around ten or eleven.

It was clear to Luke that, for once, he was not the only one who could see the children as everyone was silent, mouths

Chapter 15: Full Circle

dropped wide open in awe. "It is a privilege they only reserve for a special few," one whispered excitedly. Even those who may have seen them before, such as past relic seekers, could not hide the look of amazement on their faces. "All thirteen children at once," someone whispered. Everyone waited with baited breath to hear what the children had come to say and what would happen next.

The oldest child began to speak, the others joined in harmoniously. The strangest thing was that although all the children's mouths moved, only the oldest actually spoke. Even stranger still was the fact that the voices of all thirteen children came from just that one child. This child spoke for the rest, in the most literal sense.

"We thank you, you have achieved what has needed to be done. Only one thing remains. As you have been informed before the relic must be returned to its original temple; that temple is not here. The hallowed temple is atop this very mountain, nestled in the extinct volcanic crater." They spoke to Luke directly now, "Bring us the relic, seeker, you must complete this final task as it was once foretold. Serve us well."

"He shall do it," Fredrick announced after performing a full deep bow in-front of the children, not giving Luke the chance to speak.

The children smiled. They then began to shimmer and

Surface

become translucent, as the relics had before. They continued to fade before completely vanishing, with the exception of one child. The remaining child was the same ginger haired boy who had helped Luke to find the courage to pull through after the horrors of battle. The Hammerites appeared not to see this child as they had become deeply involved in conversation, oblivious. The boy looked directly at Luke and appeared to wipe a tear from his face before he too vanished.

Luke could not believe it, he thought his ordeal was over. He thought he could stay in his home now, but yet again it fell to him to be, well, let's face it, an overrated delivery boy. He had enough of these secrets and daft missions, he was going to march right up to Fredrick and tell him to stuff that relic where the sun don't shine. But then… he thought, maybe if he was to do this, then he could turn this situation to his advantage. After all, the children had said that he must be the one who returns the relic, so they had no other choice then to go with whatever he asked for. He certainly was in a strong bargaining position.

So Luke wasted no time, he had many things he required…

"If I am to do this…," Luke paused and made sure his gaze was fixed on Fredrick ,"Then I want no more to do with the Hammers or any of your ilk though I wish to retain the privileges they are granted and be able come and go as I

Chapter 15: Full Circle

please."

"Done," Fredrick said, almost too easily.

"I also want Aaron to be released and allowed to stay if he chooses."

There was a pause this time before Fredrick replied, "I cannot let him stay." There was a pause, "but he will be released as I promised."

Luke was annoyed. How could they deny him this simple request? he thought. He would be changing everyone's life for the better, what is more he had already been through such an ordeal already.

"Then I will not move." Luke sat down on the chair with his legs crossed. The others glared at him, who was he not to do what the children demanded?

"...Fine," Fredrick finally said after they had been glaring at each other for some time. "Complete the task and we may consider it. For now, I will allow him to aid you in your task of returning the relic."

Luke wondered if he actually wanted Aaron's help, though it pained him to think it. He knew in truth that Aaron would be more likely a hindrance than a help due to his injuries. But, on the other hand, he could not leave him

Surface

here at the Hammerites mercy, who knows what they would do to him. Luke nodded in agreement

"One more thing," Luke said.

"What is it?", Fredrick said with a sigh.

"I want to see Antheria too before I leave."

"But of course," Fredrick said rather too politely, as if he had been expecting this request.

"If we are done then? Good," Fredrick said again without giving Luke the time to reply.

"You will leave immediately. Aaron will be escorted and meet you at the exit. We know he is not trustworthy, but his skills may be valuable. skills he should be able to put to use once more now that we have helped him with his injury."

Luke did not know that they possessed the kind of technology to do that, but if they did, and they had indeed, healed Aaron, then Luke's trepidation about Aaron joining was for nothing. "Aaron should be back to his old self again, injuries healed," Luke thought.

The party walked up the spiral walkway that circled the chamber. Fredrick led the way, holding the combined

Chapter 15: Full Circle

mass of the relics, a smooth metallic sphere. It sported no designs or any other markings of any kind. The remarkable thing was that the combined weight of those relics should mean that the sphere must weigh as much as a large boulder, but Fredrick seemed to carry the sphere with ease.

They reached the end of the walkway. Luke expected Fredrick to turn left and take the lift to the surface, however they turned right and exited from where they came, through the main doors. Once again Luke was faced with those dreaded stairs. After another exhausting climb, they reached the last landing before the top. Fredrick stopped. He gestured to Luke and two of the other Hammerites to wait there while the others continued on up.

Once the others had vanished from sight, Fredrick shifted the sphere to one side with his left hand and removed a small key from within his clothing with his right. He proceeded to the innocuous looking door and unlocked it. When the door opened a cool breeze blew through as if all of the outside world was trying to rush in through this one small doorway. The wind continued to blow until the door was shut behind them once more. Now in complete darkness, one of them fumbled for a light switch. A click was heard and a florescent light above buzzed into life. One by one lights all the way down the passage came to life in a similar fashion, illuminating a long passage in a

Surface

flickering halogen glow. Luke could see no end to the passage, it seemed to go on forever into the distance. It was as if he was staring into a pair of mirrors set parallel to each other so that they reflected each other's reflection into infinity.

After more than an hour walking along the corridor all of which was on a slight uphill gradient, they came to a rock fall. Luke was glad for the change of pace, though the perilous rocks did get his heart racing as he slowly wormed his way between them, trying hard as he possibly could not to touch anything. The corridor continued beyond the fall where they came upon more and more rock falls. Climbing over the top of these allowed them to continue. Side passages began to branch off, with nothing but darkness filling them, hiding whatever secrets and perils that might lay beyond. They passed these with caution.

Finally, after they had been walking for well over three hours, Luke could see that the end was in sight, a staircase led up. The steps, half decayed, were constructed from iron that was now in various stages of rusting metal. They followed the dubious stairs up the inside of an old mine shaft. Each step they took made the old stairs creak and moan.

Thankfully, the staircase was not too long and they emerged from it into a reasonable sized mined out

Chapter 15: Full Circle

chamber, where metal roof support beams criss-crossed between four large and solid central steel columns. The columns rose upwards into the roof, vanishing out of sight. In the middle of the four columns sat an old lift cage, partially enclosed with no roof. Surrounding the lift and columns was an ageing wooden platform that stank of decay. One of the Hammerites put his foot right through the platform when he climbed up.

With everyone assembled in the chamber, the two guards turned and left, leaving Fredrick and Luke alone. Luke did try to strike up a conversation with Fredrick, mainly out of sheer boredom, but the man was just not interested. Maybe Fredrick was still seething due to all of demands that were made of him earlier, Luke thought. After a bit more of a wait they could hear the unmistakable noise of boots on metal and the metal protesting in return. Aaron emerged, escorted by several guards. Luke could see that Aaron was heavily laden with not just one but two backpacks, one of which Luke recognised as his own, taken from his home.

Aaron waved to Luke, making sure to show him his previously injured hand. Luke was amazed that he counted five fingers where there had been two fingers and three stumps. Luke had already been told that Aaron injuries had been treated, but he still had to give Aaron's hand a double take. When Aaron moved close enough it took Luke a few moments to deduce that Aaron had in fact been given highly convincing prosthetic fingers. Not only did the fingers look real, but they also seemed provide a degree of movement though they appeared somewhat limited in speed and flexibility. Aaron would never be a speed typist, but it was certainly an improvement on before.

Luke hoped that Antheria would be among those escorting Aaron, but she was not. When asked, Fredrick simply said that someone had been despatched for her, but it was up to her to decide whether to come or not. Maybe she was not coming then, maybe she was annoyed with Luke, but why? Well maybe, Luke thought, it was for the simple fact that he would be leaving her, again. Not fair, he thought, not like he had much choice in the matter.

Fredrick grew impatient and handed Luke the sphere forcibly. Grasping it, Luke immediately could tell why Fredrick had handled it with such ease. It weighted almost nothing, he feared it might float away if he did not keep a tight grip. Strangely, despite its light weight, it felt and sounded solid. What strange metals was this constructed from and where had did all the mass of the combined relics gone? Yet another mystery born of the children.

Aaron climbed into the elevator, brandishing his new prosthetic fingers with a smile. Yet Luke did not follow and instead remained on the old wooden platform. A while later, and after badgering from all concerned, he

Chapter 15: Full Circle

finally relented and turned to enter the lift. He stopped again to everyone's dismay and turned away from the cage once more, he heard Antheria's voice. She and Jason emerged panting from another tunnel leading off from the chamber.

"Luke," she called, afraid she would miss him once more.

"I will not lose you again," she shouted.

Luke did not respond. He could not ignore the fact that it was Jason who escorted her.

"I have to do this," he eventually yelled back as he glared at Jason. He knew she would turn to him in his absence. His anger was starting to boil, not only was he to risk his life with this task, he might lose her too. He focused his anger at the sphere held in his hand the current source of his problems. He had to stop himself from throwing it away right there and then.

"Then I will come with you," Antheria shouted.

It was as if a pressure valve had been released on one of the geothermal steam pipes and Luke's simmering rage quickly dissipated as the steam would have. Luke had never considered this, but he soon wondered, why not? Was it because he was being sexist? No, he knew Antheria could look after herself. To have her with him would

Surface

actually be a dream come true. On the other hand, where they were going, to the top of this mountain, could be spell disaster for them both. He could be bringing her with him to their mutual death!. There was something else too, deep down within him, something that was trying tell him, no, she cannot come. Something wanted to make him yell: "No, go home, Antheria!"

Luke once again looked at Jason, who seemed to look rather smug as he stood there, for Jason knew once Luke had gone he could make his move. This was enough for Luke, he held out his hand for Antheria and beckoned her to join him. She did not hesitate and ran up onto the wooden platform and into the lift, sending dust flying from the old platform as she ran. Jason did not follow, he could see that Antheria had made her choice. Luke held Antheria's hand and together they pulled the lever that began their ascent, while Aaron rolled his eyes and tutted to himself. The lift chains became taught and the fragile cage began to rise.

Chapter 16: Passageways

After the first few feet of painfully slow progress, the lift jerked and the rate of ascent increased. Despite the speed increase, the lift still appeared to be travelling at only a slightly faster pace than that of a snail, so that it now matched the speed of an ant. They slowly left the chamber behind. The small cage rattled and clanged its way up the shaft. The lift randomly jerked and swung from side to side, occasionally crashing into its guide rails. None of them felt particularly safe in this ancient contraption.

Eventually it calmed down and ceased its wild movements, doing everyone's hearing and nerves a favour. It grew darker with the chamber now all but a faint glow below them, which was their only light source. Soon even that glow was gone, and they were now in total darkness, not even the most avid carrot eater would be able to see now. Luke fidgeted, he could simply not stay still. He constantly felt as if he was going to fall over in the dark. The darkness and the drop seemed all too familiar, it was just like his earlier dream. The thought of falling was now all he could think about. Luke sat, or more like fell, to the floor of the cage, to try and shake off the dizziness this was causing.

"You been drinking?," Aaron asked after hearing the thud.

Surface

"Feels like it." Luke replied. "Do me a favour, pass me my pack."

Aaron frowned before reluctantly handing Luke his pack, it had made a comfy chair. Luke rummaged through his things, he hoped the stuff that he had packed all that time ago, before making his ill fated journey to tunnel 4W was still there. It took some time, but he eventually found what he was looking for. As he removed the item from his pack there was a loud crash, the rusty lift found its guide rails once more. This brought him back to reality, the mere act of rummaging had taken his mind off things. He had almost forgotten that he was travelling in an ancient rusty basket now suspended hundreds of feet above the ground. He was also lucky not to drop it.

He held the device and switched it on. Light beamed out from the device, the device being an electronic torch. Using that light he was able to locate another two in his backpack. He then handed them out to Antheria and Aaron. Aaron was at first puzzled by the device. He had turned it on by mistake and it shone directly into his face startling him, and he too almost dropped it down the shaft.

With all their lights on they could now see the rusty guide rails and the beams that made up the shaft. Disturbingly many of these beams were bent or broken. Every fifty feet or so, tunnels led off into the darkness, each one with their own marking. The first one they saw read "L37", the next

Chapter 16: Passageways

passage up read "L36", and so the sequence continued.

As they continued to explore their surroundings with their lights, their silhouettes were randomly cast upon the shaft's walls. Aaron could see that this was making everyone nervous in this eerie and dark place, so he decided to amuse everyone by changing those shadows into anything his imagination could come up with, by making shadow puppets. Aaron had plenty of practice, he would often use this to entertain himself on those long torch lit journeys down the Red Way.

Antheria did a particular good impression of a startled cat when the lift came to a sudden stop with an almighty crash. There, three inches above Aaron's was the tapered end of broken beam that now extended into the lift cage from the shaft wall. If the beam had not stopped the lift, Aaron would have surely been skewered. Their upward journey had been stopped.

"What now?" all three of them asked almost in unison. They looked around the dark shaft. By a sheer fluke, they noticed that they had stopped just several feet from one of the passages leading off. The passage was marked "L11".

There was a squeal of metal and the lift jerked and moved upwards by an inch. The sounds of metal protesting filled their ears as the lift strained to move itself again, only to be stopped by its guide beams as the lift tilted. The beams

Surface

started to give and the lift tilted more severely; the carriage now lurched to one side. Metal around the beam twisted further, the lift was desperate to continue on its upwards journey. They had no other choice, they had to get out and make a try for the passage as the lift likely would disintegrate under the strain.

It was possible to climb the cage's gate and then through the hole made by the intruding metal girder. From there, they could climb into the passageway. Aaron climbed up first, he almost fell as he was still not used to his new fingers. Nevertheless he made it safely onto the girder. Luke and Antheria passed their packs to Aaron, and he threw them into the passage above. Antheria climbed up next aided by Luke from the bottom and Aaron from above. The help was welcome, though it was not needed. Antheria climbed past Aaron and then on into the passage. Aaron held out his hand for Luke to come up.

The lift jerked violently again and Luke lost his footing, falling to the floor. Frantically he stood up again. He managed to jump and grab onto Aaron's hand, just as the gate in-front of him was ripped from its hinges and crashed down the shaft. Luke now dangled in mid-air with only Aaron's hand holding him aloft. The lift, now free of the girder, swung back in the opposite direction. The roof of the cage forced its way between their arms and Luke was wrenched from the safety of Aaron's grip.

Chapter 16: Passageways

Luke was thrown back and violently crashed into the rear of the cage, almost wholly head first. Luke went limp and collapsed motionlessly on the floor. This was the last thing they saw of him before the lift roared upwards as if pulled by a tensioned spring.

"No!," Antheria screamed in its wake.

"Luke," Aaron called too.

Antheria began to sob, she could not help herself, so Aaron attempted to console her. "He will be al right, he's probably just knocked out," he said.

"But…," Antheria fretted. She was losing him, again. Luke was being whisked away to the surface without her, just like before.

"He'll be al right," Aaron repeated. "He's too daft to do anything stupid."

Antheria was not amused with that jest, regardless of the fact it was actually said to make her feel better. She let it go for now.

She resolved herself not to let herself go through it all again, forever wondering if she ever would see Luke again. No, this time she was going to do something about it, she was going to find a way up and return to him.

Surface

There had to be another way up, surely? "Perhaps these levels are linked in some other way, maybe there is another lift shaft we could use?," she said out loud. Antheria stood up and immediately set off at a brisk pace down the passage through the darkness along the ancient mined level; Aaron followed in hot pursuit. The passage appeared to have decayed severely, rock laid strewn about everywhere and what had been wooden sleepers beneath an ancient railway had completely rotted away into a distant memory and only their blackened shadows remained.

They came across an alcove full of rusted, strange machinery, the purpose of which was indeterminable. They ignored this and carried on. Ahead of them they could see light, light that was not of their own making. The light shone down from above like a spotlight highlighting a performer on a stage, only in this case the performer was long dead, as the spread out pile of bleached white bones testified. The bones were broken, pulverised, in fact. Perhaps this was too extensive to be decay alone a lot of the damage was likely from a heavy impact with the floor from a great height. The remains of an old rope seemed to confirm this.

The light was daylight, but its source was but a pinprick many hundreds of feet above. There was no way to climb this shaft, there was no lift nor ladders. Any thoughts of scaling the shaft were banished by those bones; they did

Chapter 16: Passageways

not want to become like that, both dead and forgotten.

They carried along the passage.

"So Aaron, tell me about your people," Antheria said.

"I would rather not," Aaron replied.

"Why was he being so evasive, was he hiding something? Well, they did tell me not to trust outsiders," Antheria thought.

After much more pestering, Aaron did finally reveal that he was once a farmer, but that circumstances had forced him to take another route in life. But that was about as much as he was willing to divulge before quickly changing the subject again. Perhaps he did not want to tell Antheria the full truth for fear of reprisal. This, he felt, was rather out of character for him. Revealing his past would not have bothered him before. Heck, he was proud of his thieving skills and the fact he had developed them from scratch.

As they walked on they noticed that to their left was yet another shaft, however now there was finally hope because in the shaft behind the rotting timbers stood a ladder, a ladder made of metal. Despite it most likely being ancient, it looked in relatively good condition. Cautiously they both began to climb, this seemed to be their only way

up. The ladder creaked and rocked slightly, but it held
steady. The ladder ended after about one hundred feet at
the next level above. Directly across the passage in front of
them was another steel ladder leading up another shaft.
They climbed this too, as well as the three proceeding
ones, to gain almost 500 feet in height. Surely they must
be near the surface now?

Antheria was becoming tired and irritable. She just
wanted Luke back and had no time for Aaron being
Aaron. By the time they reached the fifth ladder to the
next level, Antheria began letting out her frustrations out
on poor Aaron.

"Must you comment on everything? Not everything is a
joke, Aaron!" Antheria scalded.

With that said Antheria shot across the passage ahead and
started to climb the next ladder to put some distance
between them. However, it was not long until she was
forced to come back down, as above her a large part of the
ladder was missing and it was now wedged across the
shaft. They would not be getting past that. They moved
along the passage in the direction they had been heading
before, in the hope of finding another shaft they could
climb. Not much time had passed before a wall loomed
into view, out of the darkness. The passage ended. It was
as if whoever had dug this passage had gotten here and
just given up. They had no choice but to try their luck in

Chapter 16: Passageways

the other direction, failing that they would be forced to try a new route back down in the lower levels.

They passed the broken shaft that they had tried to climb earlier to find that the passage ended this way too. However, this time it was not solid rock that blocked their progress it was instead the lack of it. A deep pit, ten foot wide, blocked their entry into the continuing passage. Carefully peering over the edge they just made out the bleached bones they had passed earlier, 500 feet below.

Looking up they could see that it was not far to the surface, maybe only a few hundred feet now. Draped down the side of the shaft was the remains of the other end of the old hemp rope they had found. It swayed in a light breeze, dangling menacingly. This is where the climbers must have fallen from, their rope most have snapped. The rope was out of reach and certainly not trustworthy.

Hope, however, was not entirely lost as stretched across the shaft were the remains of an old bridge. To say a bridge is a bit of an overstatement as only a beam of some four inches width remained. The base and railings had decayed and collapsed in ages past.

Aaron offered Antheria his hand and started to step out onto the beam, however she brushed his hand aside and stepped out in front of Aaron unaided. She was not willing to let this obstacle stop her, her determination was banishing her fear. She elegantly balanced her way along the beam, and it was not long until she had reached the other side, with not so much as a wobble.

Not wanting to be outdone, Aaron practically ran across the beam, confident in his nimbleness. However, about half way across he failed to spot a slimly patch on the beam. With his momentum there was nothing he could do to stop himself tumbling over. Luckily, his momentum was a double-edged sword as, though it caused him to fall, he fell forwards over the beam and not off the side. As he flew through the air he reached and grabbed for the beam. He did not fall entirely straight onto his stomach, his legs slid off one side to dangle below. Antheria was too far away to help, so Aaron had no choice but save himself. With a great effort he managed to swing one of his legs back onto the beam before hooking it there. He then swung the other leg up. Shaking, but reasonably safe, he crawled slowly forwards, like a hunter stalking its prey.

Once within reach, Antheria practically grabbed Aaron by the scruff of his neck and dragged the bedraggled man to the safety of the passage beyond.

Once Aaron had stopped shaking, he started to feel a new pain that was almost crippling. Its source was nothing physical, it was instead his pride that had been fatally wounded. Eventually composed again, both he and

Chapter 16: Passageways

Antheria continued onwards to the end of the passage. As they suspected it did terminate at the lift shaft, however their luck was in as just before the end of the passage there was a side passage ushering a strong breeze. They followed this breeze into a small passage leading up a gentle slope around many corners. Eventually this passage terminated in a small concrete room, a room that was lit by daylight, which entered through an open doorway. Opposite the doorway on the other side of the chamber was the mangled remains of the lift cage swinging silently in the breeze. Antheria rushed over to check on Luke, yet he was not there, and all that appeared to remain of him was a small pool of blood.

Luke came to just as the lift stopped. His torch was broken by the impact, so he had no means of producing light. He suddenly felt a sharp pain on the back of his head. He slowly moved his hand to the source of the pain and felt his moist hair, he was bleeding. The sharp pain thankfully subsided, but only to replaced with a throbbing headache and nausea. He staggered to his feet, feeling woozy and disorientated. He began to shuffle forwards with his arms outstretched in an attempt to feel for the lift's gate. There was, however, no gate as it had been ripped off, though Luke seemed to have forgotten that. On his seventh step he tried to put his foot down onto the floor, however his foot found no floor, it hung there above an unknown void. Luke quickly retracted his foot and placed it back upon solid ground before shakily retreating a few paces.

Surface

"So there is no floor in front, perhaps the lift had been stopped by another beam half way up the shaft or perhaps the lift had been sheared in two and there was a now huge void between me and the platform. Without light I have no way of knowing," he thought.

He sat back down to think about his situation, he felt dizzy again. He was not sure, but he may have even passed out momentarily. When he awoke again, he could have sworn he saw something. His heart raced and he could hear the sound of his heart pounding in the silent dark. A distinct glow began to form itself in front of him. His eyes were playing tricks on him, he thought. But then that shape grew definition until it was no longer an indistinct luminous blob, it was a shape of a girl, another child. The child said nothing; she was instead content with dancing backwards and forwards in the darkness. The girl smiled at Luke and offered him her hand, but before Luke could grab it, she withdrew the hand, turned around and danced again into the darkness. Without thinking, or perhaps forgetting where he was, he stood up again and attempted to follow her.

Both feet touched the void this time, it was too late for him to step back again. His stomach felt like it entered his mouth as he began to fall. It seemed like forever, but in truth it was only a moment. His body came to an abrupt stop as he impacted with a cold, hard floor. Sharp pains

Chapter 16: Passageways

shot through his partially healed ribs and Luke laid there groaning in pain. His body had taken yet another battering. After a while, the pain subsided, he had been winded. He slowly stood up again.

To Luke's surprise the girl was still there, she appeared as if she was somewhat amused by his fall. Was causing him to fall a deliberate act? Regardless, at least he was out of the lift, he thought, but he had no idea where he was. Once the girl had finished giggling, she silently turned around, away from Luke once more. She then seemed to reach up for something in the darkness before pulling it. With her task complete, she vanished instantly. Luke moved carefully forward towards where the child had stood, all the time he reached out and felt for more drops or obstacles in his way. He reached where he thought the child had been and his hands made contact with something solid and cold to the touch. He tapped on it, it sounded metallic. He moved his hands around hoping to find what the child had been reaching for, hoping it not to be another trick. To his right he noticed that the surface texture changed, it felt rougher. It was most likely rock or concrete. Moving his hands around further he eventually felt something protruding from the wall. It wobbled slightly as his hands explored the object.

He grabbed it and, like the child, he pulled down on what turned out to be a lever. The lever clicked and the door next to it swung wide open revealing the outside, a white

Surface

rock expanse that stretched off into the distance, bathed in pale sunlight. The light illuminated the chamber. It was a simple chamber with bare concrete walls and a single passageway leading off into the darkness. It would be pointless and impossible with no light to head down the passageway. He glanced at the wreckage of the lift. He could see how he had taken his fall. The lift was suspended above the floor, its damaged state prevented it from stopping in its proper place. The big fall he thought he had taken must have only been a couple of feet, though if he happened to had fallen backwards, down the shaft... he did not want to think about that outcome. So with the only other exit being an uninviting dark passage, he made his way out of the concrete room onto the rocky, breezy surface.

The landscape undulated like a sea frozen in a middle of a storm. There were large waves of rock some twenty or thirty feet high, fissures and cracks snaked between and through them. The air was cold and within moments Luke was forced to grab another layer of clothing from his pack. The wind was strong making even the three layers he now wore still feel inadequate.

Luke examined the horizon, beyond the sea of stone. There was mass of white and blue that streamed down the mountainside above; it was ice, the ice of a glacier. Luke knew this would be a serious obstacle to the journey upwards unless he could find a way around. The temple

Chapter 16: Passageways

he knew was at the top of the mountain above the glacier.

He started picking his way across the rock, trying to find the best route through this dangerous crack ridden terrain. His footing and his mission were the only two things on his mind. Perhaps this, coupled with the effects of a mild concussion, was why it took Luke over one hundred paces to realise that he was leaving Aaron and Antheria behind. How would they know where he had gone, if he continued?

"Should I wait? But if I do, for how long? Would they even be able get up here in the first place?," Luke questioned himself.

He decided in the end that he had to wait, at least for a little while. He returned to the relative warm of the concrete room that stuck out of the landscape like a square molehill.

He hoped that they would find another way up. There was hope of this from the side passage he noticed on his way out. Several hours passed, yet there was still no sign of them and he began to give up hope of ever seeing them again. He determined that if they did not turn up soon he would have no choice but to set out without them.

Chapter 17: The White Mountain

Aaron noticed a small trail of blood leading across the concrete before disappearing outside. This was where Luke must have gone, Aaron realised. Antheria cringed at the sight of this blood. She was no stranger to blood, injuries from geothermal pressurised explosions were a common place in her old work, it was the knowledge that this was Luke's that made her feel sick.

They moved outside and then called out for Luke, however he did not answer and could not be seen anywhere. The wind outside was fierce, and the light was fading fast. Calling out to Luke in this wind was futile. They would have to head the way they presumed he would go and hopefully pick up his trail when they reached the snow higher up, hoping not to find him collapsed or worse, dead, along the way.

They crossed over the first ravine. Aaron could have sworn he heard something nearby, beyond a large rock just in front of him. Aaron approached and cautiously began to peer around to the other side of the rock.

As Aaron moved around the rock he noticed the smell of ammonia. That was a smell he recognised from the streets; he knew what it was.

Chapter 17: The White Mountain

"Took you long enough," Luke said. "Luke!" Aaron was certainly glad he was all right and held out his hand to grasp Luke's hand in a firm and warm handshake. Before he did, however, Aaron remembered the smell and further noticed a small steam of yellow liquid running down the rock; so Aaron changed his mind on the handshake, and instead greeted Luke with a pat on the back.

"Glad to see you're al' right," Aaron said with a grin.

Antheria appeared, wondering what was happening. She too worked out why Luke was behind the rock, but as she was so glad to see him, she did not care and launched herself at him regardless before proceeding to hug and kiss the life out of him.

As she touched the back of his head, she realised it was damp. She released her embrace and then stepped around him to inspect from behind. She could see a trail of semi-dried blood leading down from a gash on the back of Luke's head into his blood soaked clothes.

She knew he was hurt from the blood at the lift, but she did not know how badly until now. Aaron realised too that Luke was hurt, so they both had practically to fight each other off to tend to Luke's wound. It turned out to be a relatively minor cut, but, like all head wounds, they tend to look far worse than they are, owing to the amount of

Surface

blood normally produced from the smallest of cuts to the scalp.

"Glad you have a thick head," Aaron said.

Luke's wounds tended, they set about setting up camp as the sun was sinking below the horizon. It would be suicidal to try and navigate this dangerous landscape at night.

They began to lay out the coverings and bedding for their shelter. "They" consisted of Luke and Antheria only. Aaron was enjoying his commanding role, probably a little too much by now. He ordered Luke and Antheria about with what he called helpful suggestions. Luke had become used to this over time, but he had hoped Aaron would go back to his usual more practical self now that he had regained a better use of his hand. Antheria, on the other hand, had only known Aaron a day so, so she had not got used to him at all. It had also had been a truly long day, so tempers were very fraught.

"Fine then!," Antheria said to Aaron in a not so "fine" way.

Antheria positioned the covering as Aaron instructed, or "suggested," into its new position. It stood firm for well over a minute before collapsing in the first strong gust of wind, just as Antheria thought it would have.

Chapter 17: The White Mountain

There was no apology from Aaron, only the response, "But you did not tie the reef knot right. Women, eh?" The last part of the statement he directed to Luke. Luke did not respond, knowing whatever he said would put him against the other, this was going to be a long trip in more ways than one, Luke thought. He still felt a little woozy and his head ached, the last thing he wanted was blazing arguments.

At Aaron's remark, Antheria kicked the thankfully empty small cooking pot from where it stood over the fire; this caused it to skitter its way across the rock surface before rolling noisily down into a nearby crevasse. With this Luke was now forced to take a role of peace keeper. The first requirement of this role was to clamber down the crack, that was thankfully shallow, to retrieve the pot. After completing that task, he then encouraged the reluctant Aaron to finish the job on the shelter himself as Luke knew he was capable of it, though admittedly he still needed help tying knots.

Overnight the temperature plummeted, but their tempers did not. There were no more violent outbursts, however, Antheria and Aaron now instead refused to talk to each other. They just sat there staring into space, trying to avoid each other's gaze. Luke wondered if it was a mistake bringing them both up here; he felt as if he was stuck with two ten-year olds. Maybe it would have been better without Aaron, Luke would have preferred to spend this time with Antheria, now they were more open with each other and not have Aaron in the way. On top of this, these arguments between Aaron and Antheria were already grating on him.

Luke decided he was too tired and too sore to contemplate the issue further and curled up under his simple bedding to get some sleep. He found getting to sleep was actually quite difficult, the cold was cutting through insufficient bedding, making his feet feel like ice blocks. This worried Luke. He knew it would be much colder the higher they went, he was not sure how he would cope. They awoke to find frost on the inside of the canvas shelter; their breath had frozen on the surface of the material like a thin layer of white dust.

Antheria and Aaron were still as cold to each other as was the air surrounding them, but as the sun came out and warmed the rock, their feelings warmed also. They were still not on good terms with each other, but at least they spoke again. Granted, most of the time it was only a few words said curtly, but still it was progress on the previous night.

Breakfast was one of the few luxuries they could enjoy, a nice juicy steamed fish sat waiting to be devoured on their plates. Luke had tried to lighten the mood by cooking this meal, but also he prepared it as a practicality. The fish goes off, quickly, even if it is a white eyeless subterranean

Chapter 17: The White Mountain

"ghost" fish. Luke did not mention that this would be their last luxury and from now on their meals would consist of small portions of cured dry meat, hardy long lasting vegetables, and plenty of bread that would be stale by journey's end.

They looked outside their shelter, the weather had changed for the worse. The sky was now entirely white as fog had descended, dropping the visibility down to less than a hundred feet. Navigation would be difficult and dangerous on this terrain. Luke had a compass, which he thoughtfully glanced at the previous night and noted the direction of the glacier to be south by south-east. However, even with this tool finding the temple would still be difficult. Once they climbed the glacier, then what? The mountain could be part of a range of several peaks. One would have thought the children would have given them more precise guidance, but as always they were vague.

Luke re-imagined the children's instructions in a satirical manner: "Hey, just head to the temple at the top of the mountain. It's the first one on your right, you can't miss it. If you fall to your death, then you have gone too far."

They packed up their belongings and layered up with furs on top of furs. The air was colder than the last day and snow began to fall. The journey was problematic from the start. As the snow grew deeper, it began to hide the cracks and ravines, almost causing several falls. They eventually

Surface

decided to tie each other together using Aaron's rope before continuing; this delay made them even colder. Tying knots is most difficult when your digits don't work due to the cold.

Briefly the sky cleared, allowing them a glimpse of the foot of the glacier, which was now far closer and appeared menacing. Its sheer ice walls seemed to be an impossible barrier. To the right, however, there was the possibility of a way on, a steep partially snow covered scree slope. It would still be a difficult route, but not impossible. It was their only choice as they had no ice axes or crampons to traverse the glacier with. Luke took a compass bearing before the glacier was once again hidden from view. Navigation, thankfully, had always been one of Luke's strong points.

Onwards they went, following the compass blindly as if being led by the hand of an invisible stranger. They did not know exactly where they would end up, or if they would even ever get there.

The constant meandering around holes and rocks in the fog meant that there was even less of a chance that Luke would get his bearings right. Then the scene in front of them grew darker and soon the gloom of the mist was replaced by towering ice walls of the glacier that were impossible to climb. They took a chance that the slope was to the west and followed the bottom of the creaking

Chapter 17: The White Mountain

glacier. It only took a short walk before the walls of ice were replaced by a steep slope of rock and snow. Even Luke was amazed with himself that he had only been a few hundred feet out.

Before they even set foot on the slope, the instability of it became apparent as small pebbles bounced their way down as if reacting to them merely looking at it. Nevertheless they began their perilous and tiring ascent. Beneath them, the ground shifted, causing them to slide half a step backwards to every step forwards they took. All too often they would progress quite far only for one of them to slip, causing them all to fall and slide down some distance. Injuries on the moving floor were minor due to their thick fur padding, but they were mounting.

Worse now, the weather was growing more severe. The wind was now biting cold and snow was falling sideways, battering them and thoroughly covering the slope. It was not long until they were in the midst of a full-blown blizzard. The storm threatened not just to freeze them to death, but it also threatened to blow them off the very mountain.

Painfully and slowly they pushed on regardless, the only other choice was to turn back in failure. That idea seemed sensible to Aaron. "To heck with this mission," he was beginning to think. He was considering why he was there in the first place. "Loyalty?" Hmm it was strange to him

Surface

that he even felt that, he had never been loyal to anyone before. Still, was this enough for him to stay?

The feeling in their fingers and toes had gone entirely, yet their calves were burning as if red-hot coals were being pressed against their legs. Luke now could tell from the glum look on Aaron's face that he wanted to turn back, and it would not be long before Antheria would likely think the same too

"Just a little further," Luke promised them hollowly, looking up when the air cleared, it did not seem that far. Soon it appeared that they would be reaching the top. Disheartingly upon reaching the top, the slope immediately rose up once more behind. The slope seemed never ending. Aaron, who had still plodded on regardless, finally stopped, "No more mate, I may be daft, but this is suicide". Luke would agree, but halfway up a mountain was no place to stop. It would be impossible to set up camp here, even worse they could not even turn back as going down in these conditions would be particularly difficult and likely deadly, especially if at night.

So Luke spelt it out "There is only one choice. either we reach the temple or some sort of shelter, or die here in the elements," Luke shouted as the wind raised in power, as if to prove his point.

Luke grabbed Aaron by his good hand and pulled him up

Chapter 17: The White Mountain

the slope. Antheria even helped to push him from behind. Thankfully after ten paces or so this proved to be enough of a motivation to get Aaron moving on his own again, mainly as it made him feel embarrassed for his moment of weakness. Luke, however, knew, that deep down Aaron was right. They would have to stop and soon it would not be possible to withstand the sheer exhaustion and exposure for much longer without rest.

The slope changed from small pebbles under the snow to large boulders strewn about in a haphazard fashion. These presented a new challenge. They had to concentrate, which was a hard feat in their condition to navigate the rocky maze; be it over or around, they clambered on. Thankfully the large rocks were far more stable than the scree, but nevertheless they were just as tiring. They came upon a pile of rocks resting against each other in such a way that they created an arch, an arch that might just be big enough for them all to shelter in. At least now they could rest and wait out the weather and contemplate their next move.

Antheria, new to daylight, was the first to notice that it was fading; they had spent almost the entire day on this slope. They shivered in their hiding place, where they managed to make a small fire out of carbide that Luke had brought from his home. With this, they managed to cook a meager meal before they would all try and get some sleep.

Surface

The next morning the weather was no better. With proper rationing, they would have food and fuel that would last for another two weeks. However, once that ran out they would be in trouble as it was highly unlikely there would be anything to hunt in the desolate landscape that surrounded them. Water, however, was in plentiful supply provided they had fuel to melt the snow with.

They spent that day huddled together in their small and unstable rock shelter. Stones often fell through the gaps, showing them how unstable their refuge had become. One wrong move from any of them and their refuge could become their tomb. But move they must as the cold whistled through the cracks, causing each of them to try and shuffle around to try and avoid the numerous streams of cold wafting air as the weather roared on.

The bickering between Aaron and Antheria continued also, mainly because Antheria was not impressed with Aaron's wit, or his stories, thinking him a brigand. In that respect, she was probably not far wrong, but Antheria did not know Aaron like Luke did. Yes, his humour could be grating, but as for his past, Luke could understand why Aaron had done the things he'd done. Luke might have done the same if he was in the same situation, Luke knew how tough life was here on the outside. Luke, though, endeavoured to remain silent when any bickering started. After all the often comical bickering was his only form of entertainment in the bolt-hole that they all shared.

Chapter 17: The White Mountain

Despite understanding Aaron, Luke could not help wishing Aaron had not come along. Though Aaron was doing nothing directly to annoy Luke, his mere presence was disrupting him from pursuing his personal goals with Antheria.

Another day came and went; the winds were still howling and the snow was still falling. The snow was getting so thick it now threatened to seal them in. Despite not moving they never felt rested, the cramped conditions and severe cold saw to that.

As night fell on the second day in their hole, the winds took on a new ferocity like they had never seen or heard before. The noise was tremendous, and there was something else too, a strange sound was carried on the wind.

"Hear that?," Aaron asked

"No," Antheria said curtly, "Now kindly remove your elbow from my side"

"Sorry," Aaron replied.

Eventually on the third day, with their legs aching, not just from the earlier climb but from their uncomfortable shelter, they finally decided that they needed to push on, regardless of the weather. The winds had eased, but it was still extremely cold, and fog now clung to the mountain, which meant even without the falling snow the visibility was still almost zero.

They slowly returned to the climb they started three days ago. The angle of the terrain started to get shallower and before long it had levelled out entirely. Had they finally reached the top? Had they sheltered in that uncomfortable bolt-hole when the end was so close?

The questions were not immediately answered as the fog from the clouds they were in blocked their view. All that they could see around them was white, they now traipsed on blindly in the snow.

"Its good, this," Aaron said, possibly sarcastically.

Luke and Antheria looked at each other, puzzled.

"I should do this more often, this is a cheap way of getting drunk. My head is spinning." The altitude, cold and exhaustion were all taking their toll on them, but it seemed to effect Aaron the worst. The elements did not relent and conditions grew worse as snow began to fall again and the bite of the cold air deepened.

Luke was on the limits of exhaustion too, but he could tell that Aaron was even worse. He decided to strike up a

Chapter 17: The White Mountain

conversation with Aaron, simply to get their minds off their current predicament. Luke rolled his eyes trying to think of something, but he could think only of the cold and his aching body. He wondered again, why he was doing this. More significantly, why was Aaron?

Aaron did say he hoped there would be relics to plunder. Wealth did seem to be the main driving force behind Aaron's actions so this could be true. However, Luke refused to believe that, he knew there had to more behind his motivations. No one would put themselves through this just for that surely? What was driving him?

With all of them wondering this, a conversation was stuck up between them all. Aaron restated it was the riches that drove him and Luke was forced to leave it at that. Antheria steered the conversation in a different direction in order to get them to list their greatest wants, which would hopefully give them that extra little strength to continue.

For Antheria, all she wanted was to feel warm, she wanted the comfort of her bed that and a cup of hot chocolate, a rare commodity underground.

Luke, when asked, had to think a little more. He too wanted to be home, if only so he could escape the cold. He recalled being content as he sat in his room looking through all the media he had found of the world before the ice. He recounted to them both how these items allowed him to escape the dull authoritarian world he lived in. One imagining he said sat in his mind now in particular. He would think of himself sat next to a babbling stream lazily dangling a line. He imagined the warmth of a bright sunlit day beating down on his back, oh how he wanted warm again too.

For Aaron, it was not rolling in riches as how they would have expected him to answer. It was instead the feel of warm amber mead slipping down his gullet, sat in-front of a roaring fire.

The conversation must have been working because Luke certainly was beginning to feel warmer, the feeling was even returning to his extremities, painfully.

In front of them the terrain ceased to be bland and featureless. The fog was lifting to reveal a criss-cross of shadows. The source of the shadows? Large towering ice pinnacles some of which were at least thirty feet tall, most likely carved by the savage mountain winds.

A strange moaning noise reverberated around the icy pinnacles. Luke froze in place, almost literally. It may have been the same sound Aaron heard the previous day, only this time they could all clearly hear it. The moan, as he could best describe it, was high pitched yet complemented by a low pitch rumble. Perhaps it was just the trick of the wind as it played on the ice?

Chapter 17: The White Mountain

Luke resumed walking forwards, carefully meandering between the ice. He noticed that the wind had almost died away completely, and it was definitely warmer than before too. Ahead beyond the ice he could see blue sky, the cloud was breaking.

Luke spotted something strange in the distance:

"Is that, no, it can't be, not this high up?"

However, Luke's curiosity of what lay on the horizon abruptly ceased when right next to him an ice tower collapsed, sending chunks of ice sliding across the snow, one almost knocking him off of his feet. Luke looked at the stump of ice trying to find the cause of the collapse, yet he could see nothing… Except strangely the shadow of the ice pillar remained. It was as if the laws of physics somehow no longer applied. Then the shadow moved! He now saw the source as it towered above him.

It was a gigantic creature which was almost entirely white except in places where the background was not. The colours of its fur and skin changed with every movement, so it looked almost exactly the same as its environment, matching whatever was on either side of it. Luke's eyes were drawn away from its body, for the beast had opened its mouth. Its teeth were grinning back at him. These teeth were some six inches long and needle-like. Fixated, Luke almost failed to notice that the creature had raised its spiked front claws. He also almost failed to notice the length of these great limbs.

The creature threw its appendages down at Luke. He dodged instinctively and dropped to the floor before rolling to the side just as the limbs crashed to the floor, making vast gouges in the snow. It raised its limbs again, Luke did not know which way to roll. He did not have to, the creature lumbered about face to find the source of a new irritation. Antheria had drawn the creature's full attention. It turned to strike her.

Chapter 18: The colour of Autumn

Aaron had stopped upon hearing the sound, his eyes scanned the ice towers for its source as Luke progressed between them. He saw nothing, but his instincts were telling him otherwise; there was something here. To the left of Luke the ice tower collapsed, and Aaron's eyes suddenly recognised a shape that was not there before. What lay before him could only be described as a cross between a polar bear and a praying mantis. The bear made up the creature's body while the praying mantis made up the creature's head and limbs.

The creature was heading straight for Luke; Aaron had not even the time to shout a warning before the creature pounced upon Luke. Luke dropped down and dodged its attack. The creature stood still, ready to bear down on Luke. With the short lack of movement the creature's camouflager was again in sync with its surroundings, making it virtually impossible to see.

Aaron instinctively raised and readied his bow, aiming at what he thought was the creature. Aaron could not feel his fingers, but it was not just the cold, of course. He now realised that the prosthetic fingers made the delicate art of precise aiming very difficult, in an instant he realised he was no longer the crack shot he once was.

Surface

He had to shoot, there was no choice as it would kill Luke before moving on and devouring him and Antheria as side dishes. He tried to steady his aim but struggled; shivering made it even worse. He drew his bow string back, yet another task he found almost impossible as his arms now joined in with the rest of his body to cry out in pure exhaustion. His arms trembled even more violently as the string reached his chin.

He loosed, the arrow seemed to curve to the left towards Antheria before swinging back again. Then it stopped in mid-flight! An oozing liquid trickled out of where the arrow had stopped, indicating that he had hit the target. The creature, however, seemed to be barely effected and made only a slight yelping sound. He would have to strike it in the head, a tall order considering the creature was camouflaged, and Aaron could barely even grip the bow string, but nevertheless he had to try. The creature became visible again as it had now turned to Antheria, thinking her the person responsible for the arrow. She did the most sensible thing one can do in this sort of situation, she ran. The creature pursued her rapidly carelessly knocking over various ice pinnacles as it went, sending them crashing down like glass dominoes.

Antheria tripped on an ice block and fell. The creature saw its chance and raised its forearms to strike as it had when it attacked Luke. Aaron's arms quivered and shook even more before he loosed a second arrow. This arrow

Chapter 18: The colour of Autumn

just missed Antheria and instead struck the snow beside her. The creature impaled its limbs upon the place where Antheria would have been, had she too not rolled to the side. The creature soon learned to counter this move and changed its tactics. It pushed its head towards Antheria, while its claws surrounded her, pinning her in place; its jaws slid open ready to devour her. Aaron readied another arrow and loosed. This one struck the creature and made enough of an impact for it to let out an almighty roaring squeal. It staggered backwards into several more ice columns, the whole area was looking like a site of a meteor impact. It was enraged now. It charged directly forward at Aaron, Aaron retrieved another arrow from his quiver.

A pain in his abdomen and the wind being knocked out of him meant he was too slow in releasing the arrow; his exhausted arms were just not fast enough, He was not fast enough.

"Damn my arms, damn my fingers," he thought as he lay there, about to be eaten.

He felt warm liquid run down his cheek; the creature appeared to be drooling, most likely in anticipation of tucking into his flesh. Then there was another squeal and Aaron realised that the liquid was not drool it was blood, the creature's blood, the source of which was a hole in the creature's skull made by his own arrow. When the creature crashed into Aaron, the sheer force of the impact must have caused him to loose the arrow unintentionally right into the creature's skull, no, it was its eye.

The creature staggered. It was not dead, but the injuries he had inflicted on it was enough to make it flee. Now almost entirely invisible, it was gone in mere seconds. The pain in Aaron's stomach sharpened and his own red blood joined the creature's in staining the snow. Luke rushed over to his aid.

"Its not that bad," Luke said.

A shiver ran down Aaron's spine, he knew that these words were often used to comfort the dying. A tear ran down Aaron's face. It froze before it even reached his cheek bone.

"No, really, It's not that bad," Luke repeated.

Aaron looked down at the wound, Luke was right. His armour had taken most of the blow, but there was still quite a deep cut below the belly button. Considering how severe the wound could have been, it was in reality relatively minor. It certainly was not life threatening, provided it was treated before infection would set in. Luke was no medic, but Aaron was able to instruct him in all the necessities so that his wound was treated correctly.

Chapter 18: The colour of Autumn

Luke realised that Aaron had saved him again and wished he had never even considered the possibility of sending Aaron away, Luke would have to repay him. For now, however, the best he could do was to finish dressing the wound and help Aaron to his feet. Antheria too decided to let the past bickering be bygones, with this act she truly saw the normally hidden selfless side to Aaron.

Once their hearts had stopped racing, and their breath was caught, they could now begin to investigate the increasingly intriguing horizon. It was not white or grey but was black, black bare rock. Strangely, they could make out spots of green. Was there life up here?

They wandered cautiously towards the black rock, meandered between the remaining ice pinnacles. All of them kept a wary eye and ear out for the creature or anything else; one could jump out at any moment. Even the slightest sign of movement caused them all to flinch and reach for any weapons they had at hand.

The ice below their feet had melted away, they were now walking on dark basalt rock. The rock rose up in front of them to form a low long circular ridge. It was clear that those green spots were indeed plants, shoots of crab grass, most likely the hardy kind of flora that are only found in the mountains. The temperature appeared to have risen dramatically though so that for the first time in perhaps a week they were actually sweating, they even had to remove several layers of clothing. Luke and Aaron both tried to discreetly examine Antheria's form as she swapped her clothes for lighter ones. When she got to her bottom layer, Luke politely turned away quickly, though Aaron did not.

"So those were plants I saw, how can it be this hot?," Luke said partly in an effort to snap Aaron out of staring. Now facing away from Antheria he could see the blizzard from which they emerged was still raging.

"This is.... well, amazing," he said, ponderously

"I don't like this," Antheria said bluntly, as she had finished changing and turned to see what Luke was staring at.

"Well, at least we are warm now," Aaron chirped up, quite correctly. However, with this warmth came pain as sharp shooting pains blasted their way through Aaron's remaining fingers. An uncontrollable grimace appeared on Aaron's face as he did his best not to yell out in pain. It was clear now in the bright light that Aaron's fingers had succumbed to frost bite. His digits were red, swollen and painful, but not black, so he was lucky. If he had remained engulfed by the blizzard for much longer, he might have lost even more fingers, or worse died from the blood poisoning. As it was, however, his remaining fingers should recover after a few days provided he warmed them correctly. His swollen fingers were just another injury to

Chapter 18: The colour of Autumn

add to the many he already possessed, and any resulting scaring would be more memories of the journey.

Aaron rubbed his hands together vigorously as they climbed up to the top of the ridge. They quickly realised that this ridge formed a circle, an outer wall for a huge crater. This was no mountain this was a volcano, a volcano that might still be active.

"That may explain the heat," Luke thought. The heat was most certainly welcoming, but he did not fancy the idea of being burned alive by molten lava.

One thing that Luke could not rationally explain was the plant life that filled the crater, the likes of which none of them had ever seen before or even imagined. Even more amazing was the structure in the centre of it all, an unnatural arrangement that could only be the children's great temple. The temple's dimensions were mind boggling; it had two large spires that stretched into the sky for what they guessed was over a kilometre. Both spires leaned at an odd angle of about seventy-five degrees. The construction below the towers was also at an odd angle, maybe it had partially subsided on one side. How old was this place, they both wondered. Other details of the building were not clear from this distance as they gazed at the odd, partially rectangular shape in the distance. They could tell, even from this distance, that the temple did not appear to be made of stone or any material that either of

Surface

them was familiar with. Its colour was black as the darkest night sky, and it reflected no light.

They slid and climbed their way down the ridge, sending stones scattering and cascading as they went. They reached the bottom and entered the surreal landscape and got up close to the strange unknown flora. Spread in-front of them were plants of yellow, purple and orange that gave the whole place the look of a deciduous forest on an autumn's day, an autumn forest, that is, if viewed by a mad man!

The plants they could see did not conform to natural laws that govern any flora they knew about. The main thing that stood out was that normally plants do not get up and move about, but these did! Take the purple plants for example. At rest they almost appeared to be heather, but if threatened or if they had exhausted their food/water supply, they would pull up their roots, and form into balls like tumble weed and move using seemingly intelligent thought to find a new place to set down their roots again.

The yellow plants were at least stationary, but were both solid and rigid like metal bristles on a scouring brush, which stood two to five feet tall. Luke approached one, but quickly jumped away when the one closest to him grew to more than twice its original height in mere milliseconds, skewering a passing bird as it did so. The remains of the bird slowly dribbled down the plant to be collected and

Chapter 18: The colour of Autumn

presumably digested by the leaves of the plant.

The orange plants were much like the grass they were used to, but as they stepped onto it, it changed colour, changing from orange to a shade of blue. The plants in the area around them immediately did the same, as if reacting to their presence. The colour change cascaded its way through different species of plants like a giant shock-wave for several meters in every direction. The flowers in the grass closed up and slipped away into the ground to hide, and the purple tumble-weed rolled away. It appeared as if the plants all shared a symbiotic defence mechanism.

Antheria could hear Luke mumbling to himself as they traversed this strange and frightening landscape. His mumblings seemed to infer that he was wondering if he was doing the right thing. He also rambled on about the children existing in such a strange place.

In a few places nothing grew at all and there was just bare, sharp, black rock in the flora's place. It was solidified lava, layered wave upon wave. This was indeed a volcanic crater. It was on one of these rocks not the dangerous plant or animal life, that felled Antheria. Tired from her journey and awe struck with the strange sights and sounds, she did look where she was going and crashed into one of these rocks. Her only saving grace was that she managed to avoid skewering herself on the yellow "impaler" plants.

Surface

Her face said it all, it was bad. She grasped her ankle in pain. It appeared that she must have landed badly. She had twisted, if not broken, her ankle. Aaron and Luke did not know this and tried to help her stand, but as soon as she put weight on it she screamed and fell back down again, adding a gash to her arm. Luke examined her ankle. It was not yet swollen, but he was sure it soon would be.

Luke was almost becoming frantic, but he still remained focused enough to deal with the problem, working on an instinct that always seemed to kick in in these sorts of moments. First, he withdrew his blade and with a grand slash he chopped down one of the spike plants. He turned the spike so that the pointed end was facing the floor and removed the tip of the spike with a flick of his blade. This he used as a rudimentary crutch. With the help of the crutch and Luke's and Aaron's shoulders, Antheria was able to at least get to her feet again. However, moving was very difficult, especially traversing through this demanding and strange terrain; she could not put weight on her ankle. Progress was excruciatingly slow. Worse still, now being unable to flee with Antheria in tow they were now even more open to attack from whatever might live here. She would make them all an easy target. Despite this, they continued to battle on, their own pains making it even more difficult.

Hours passed, yet the temple appeared to be no closer.

Chapter 18: The colour of Autumn

"Stop," Antheria demanded. Fatigued, Luke was relieved but at the same time panicking as he was thinking "What now?"

"This is stupid, we cannot continue like this," Antheria said.

"So what is the alternative?," Luke asked.

"Leave me behind," she said calmly. Luke genuinely had not considered this as an actual option, and so at first he did not take her seriously.

"What, don't be daft," Luke said,

"We will be fine," Aaron lied jokingly while panting.

Antheria's next response was very frank and to the point.

"If we continue at this speed, we will die. What have we got, five maybe six days of supplies left? How long would it take to get there at this speed? Another day, two days? Not to mention the time it would take to get back home. What of the dangers inside? You do not know what is in there, I am no help to you like this, I... I am a burden to you," she said while gazing directly into Luke's eyes.

Luke knew now that she was serious and, what is more,

she also had a particularly good point. Luke, however, still refused to believe that this was an option. He could not leave her here. Who knew what was lurking about? At least he knew he could protect her while she was with him. So he remained defiant and stated again that he would not leave her.

She insisted again. If he just managed to convince her to continue on for a little while, maybe she would change her mind.

"At least let us find somewhere safer, that is not out in the open" he said. Of course he hoped and expected to find nothing of the sort.

Begrudgingly Antheria agreed, so with that they slowly pushed on. Thankfully the plant life grew less dense, and there was little more need for bush whacking. The majority of plants they encountered were of the purple "tumble heather" variety, as Aaron called them. Thankfully it generally rolled out of their way as they approached.

They walked until the sun was starting to descend in the sky, signalling that it was mid-afternoon, and it was then when they came across an overgrown small natural cave entrance in the rock. Aaron inspected it, he could see it expanded out just beyond the entrance into a comfortably wide chamber. It was a lava tube that had collapsed only twenty feet further in, meaning he could see that there

Chapter 18: The colour of Autumn

was nothing hiding in there. There was also no evidence of any creature ever making its home in the small cave, at least nothing large; it did seem quite safe.

Antheria released herself from Luke's grip and began to crawl into the cave, Luke shouted after her.

"This will have to do," she said as she turned around and stuck her head out of the hole, being careful not to bang her injured ankle.

This was her safe haven, the haven that Luke hoped they would never actually find. Luke could still not bring him self to leave her there, so the argument they had earlier resumed anew, however, this time Aaron fought in Antheria's corner.

"She's right you know, Luke," Aaron said, as once again Antheria had restated her reasons for a third time why she should be left behind.

"But…" Luke said, unable to think of a rebuttal.

Under unrelenting pressure from both of them, Luke finally conceded defeat. He held out his hands and the two of them embraced each other in a farewell kiss. Now he knew there was no changing her mind, so he made the most of the kiss while Aaron looked on.

Surface

"I will be back by tomorrow at the latest," Luke promised.

"I know," said Antheria, and with that she crawled deeper into the hole, leaving Aaron and Luke to push on unhindered down a steepening terrain. They descended the inner rim of a second crater and reached more bare rock at the bottom. There was little life here, the whole area was enveloped by a vast shadow cast by the structure that now towered above them, a structure that was still a good distance away. The sheer scale was unbelievable. It was a wonder how anyone could have constructed it, never mind sourced the raw materials. To put it into context the highest spire must have been almost half a mile high, and the structure was estimated to be around some three miles wide. It took them another two hours before they actually reached the walls of the gargantuan temple.

Despite all of what happened Luke could not help to feel a twinge of excitement at what might come, he was living now that was for sure. He wondered what they might discover.

Up close they could see another difference between this structure and the other temples they had visited, This temple's walls were not adorned in religious symbols and relics, except for some strange protrusions, the walls were rather featureless. The structure did not even have any windows or doors, just strange spikes and outcrops

Chapter 18: The colour of Autumn

seemingly constructed at random in no discernible pattern or order. In front of them lay a huge opening with a large ramp leading down below the earth. It invited them as the jaws of a hidden predator would invite its prey. Every instinct in Aaron's body was telling him to turn around, but for now he ignored them.

The dimensions of the passage containing the ramp were again massive; this space alone could have easily held the relic chamber from Luke's home and still have room to spare. The walls, ceiling and floor were hundreds of feet apart.

As they started down the ramp, it was clear that the structure they could see on the surface was only a small part of the whole complex. It appears that the massive three-mile wide structure was only the tip of the iceberg. As they progressed they noticed even stranger things about this temple. Take the floor for instance. It appeared to be made of some kind of metal, yet the material did not act like metal. It was strange even to Luke, who was used to more advanced technology. Each step they took sounded muffled somehow, as if they were stepping on soft grass, not on solid metal.

The corridor was on a slight angle, a fact that neither of them realised, as not only did it slope downwards, it also sloped left. This made them feel slightly peculiar, as their inner ears were thrown by the angle. This made them

Surface

even tenser as they ventured on.

The daylight faded as they descended, passing through the twilight into night. The ramp levelled off somewhat, though they were still on a slight, sideways angle. It grew darker still, and they realised that the light faded far quicker than it should normally do in this immense space that was completely open at one end to daylight. They flicked on their torches and shone them ahead, and even they did not penetrate far. It was as if something was blocking the light, yet there was nothing there.

They still continued a while, though slowly, into the deepening darkness before eventually stopping due to what they could see, or more precisely what they could not see. Just in front them was darkness, tangible darkness, where all light seemed to stop. It was a wall of black, no light was reflected no surface could be seen, the blackness simply engulfed the light.

Aaron stepped back at the sight of this as he did with anything unusual a wise approach some might say. However, Luke stepped forward. He held his hand outstretched in an attempt to touch this blackness. He was close now, the light of his torch was just vanishing a mere five paces ahead. Aaron just stared at Luke transfixed, not knowing what to do. Three paces now, the hairs on Luke's arms began to stand to attention.

Chapter 18: The colour of Autumn

Aaron could stay silent no longer, his mouth began to form the shape required to shout the word stop. However, the word never came as in that nanosecond the blackness was replaced by a brilliant white. A bolt of what could only be described as indoor lightning struck Luke from the darkness. Luke made no sound and simply dropped to his knees like a stone as smoke began to stream off of him. Aaron rushed to his stricken friend's aid, but he found this action difficult as he no longer could see him; Aaron's irises had almost entirely closed due to the flash. Aaron, therefore, blundered around blindly reaching out for Luke. He eventually felt Luke's shoulders, so he grasped hard and pulled Luke back away from the black before he could be struck a second time. Aaron felt Luke shaking; at least he knew Luke was alive.

Aaron lowered Luke down into a sitting position as soon as his vision began to return to him after the bright flash. He now could see where the smoke was emanating from on Luke's person. Aaron breathed a sigh of relief, for the source of the smoke was Luke's backpack. It was that what had taken the strike, and it was still smouldering. The top of the pack was completely blackened.

Aaron removed Luke's backpack, lest it catch fire. He then checked on Luke, who was still shaking from the experience, but otherwise he seemed to have escaped the majority of the strike, if not all of it, as he had no visible injuries except for a few singed hairs on the back of his

Surface

head.

Aaron opened the backpack, though really there was no need to as the lightning had made a new entry point. Inside the pack he could see that the metal cooking implements had been turned into a molten mess, and most of the food in there had been burnt to a crisp. In the centre of all of this mess was a hole that had blasted clean through, where the contents had been apparently vaporised. At the bottom of this hole sat the relic. It glinted at Aaron as he directed his torch down onto it for a better look. He could see that it was unscathed, not a mark, nothing. The lightning had penetrated through everything in the bag only to stop at the relic. Was this what attracted the unnatural lightning?

Luke slowly began to stop shaking and after a few "crispy" jokes from Aaron he was almost back to his normal self. Luke examined the damage to his pack for himself and agreed that it must have been the relic that attracted the strike. It appeared immune to it, maybe by design. This got him thinking…

"Maybe the relic would divert the strikes to allow us to pass, or maybe it would remove the barrier altogether. Perhaps this relic was some kind of key?," Luke thought to himself silently.

When the relic had cooled sufficiently, Luke removed it

Chapter 18: The colour of Autumn

from his pack. He then studied it for a moment before holding it out in front of him, as he considered walking forwards with it held aloft. However, he soon changed his mind on this plan and instead decided to go for the safer option of rolling the relic through the blackness.

"What are you doing?," Aaron said too late as Luke had let go "Well there goes our mission," Aaron said as he watched the relic roll away.

It sounded much like a bowling ball as it travelled along, only there was not scattering of pins at the end. Instead, there were great arcs of lightning, attracted by the relic, just as Luke expected. The light was as bright as the sun; everything was lit up with one exception, the blackness itself, it remained an inky black. The light grew even more intense so that all they could see was white, just as the relics did when they were combined. Then just as quickly the lightning arcs stopped. It took a few minutes for their eyes to adjust to the resumed darkness. Luke's face sank. He could see that the blackness was still there, worse the relic was not. The relic had presumably continued to roll beyond the darkness and out of reach. Luke had lost the relic.

"That is just great, well done," Aaron said with a mocking applause. Luke normally at this point would retort with an equally sarcastic remark, but not this time.

Surface

"What was I thinking? What have I done?," The latter part he said aloud.

Their mission was over. His people would now forever live underground while he and Antheria would most likely be forced to live as outcasts. Luke would also never be rid of the children.

Luke stood up determined, maybe it was not over. He steadied his nerves for what he was about to do. He removed all metal items from his person, including his dagger and his belt that Antheria had bought him for his previous birthday. He bravely stepped forwards with his hand outstretched as he had done before.

"Have you gone wrong in the head?," Aaron questioned and protested. "Not content with throwing our mission away, you now want to throw yourself on that lightning fire too?"

"Trust me," Luke responded shakily. He flashed a smile and began to walk forwards.

Aaron did not trust Luke, but neither did he try and stop him. Luke reached the point at which all light ended and braced himself for the worst. Nothing happened, he was only a few inches from the blackness. He leaned forwards the last few inches and actually touched the darkness. There was something, but as far as he could tell it was not

Chapter 18: The colour of Autumn

actually anything physical for it had no texture and no tactile feeling at all. It was just something that prevented his hand from moving forward. He pushed harder, but his hand still refused to pass through the blackness, neither would his foot when he kicked out in frustration. He felt no pain in his toes when his foot made contact as there was nothing to kick, but the sudden jolt of his foot stopping caused pain to shoot up his tendons in his leg.

By this time curiosity had overcome Aaron's fear and there was more sound of metallic clanging as Aaron too shed all that was metal on him. He joined Luke in his attempt to pass the blackness. Aaron stared at Luke; he could see a look of anguish was evident in Luke's eyes for the relic was still beyond the barrier, and all the effort and pain they endured so far was still for nothing.

They searched the area with their torches in the vain hope that perhaps there was another way around or some kind of control. However, aside from the smooth black walls there was nothing. "But how had the relic made it through?," Aaron asked in frustration, not expecting an answer.

Luke stepped back and asked Aaron to do the same. He retrieved the melted remains of a metal spoon from the pile of metal implements on the floor. He threw it at the blackness. It got a lot closer than the relic did before, the white lightning struck it and turned it into a molten mess

Surface

on the floor. He quickly shined his torch to where he threw the spoon. The light went clean through, there was a hole, though the hole appeared to be closing.

Luke realised that the relic would have had the same if not greater effect on the barrier than the spoon. It may even have removed the barrier completely while they were momentarily blinded by the extreme light it produced. He further deduced, or hoped, that the barrier might not have fully closed yet. Luke directed his light to roughly where he had rolled the relic and sure enough, there was indeed a hole, but it was not large enough to crawl through and was shrinking further.

Aaron picked up the largest pot from the floor and without warning threw it against the blackness just above the hole made by the relic. There was an almighty crash as sparks and bolts surrounded the pot. Almost instantly it too joined the molten mess on the floor.

There was now a hole large enough to squeeze through. "After you," Aaron said, so Luke crawled through unarmed and unprepared for whatever lay ahead. A shiver went down his spine with the thought: "Maybe disarming the visitors was the intention of the barrier?"

The blackness seemed to have no thickness at all and at one point, directly underneath, Luke could see both sides simultaneously. It was like staring at the narrow edge of a

Chapter 18: The colour of Autumn

sheet of paper. He got through and stood up on the other side.

"Come through, Aaron," he called.

Luke searched for the relic or what was left of it, expecting to see a molten mess. He spotted the relic resting against a wall at the end of the passage. He examined it and could not see any obvious burns or scorches, it seemed to be fully intact.

Chapter 19: The Children Win

The space they now found themselves in was immense. Ahead, the walls and floor dropped away into more darkness, at least this appeared to be natural darkness. However, not everything was dark for there was another light source different to the one produced by their plastic torches. Looking up they could see small shafts of light beaming in through various sized holes in the roof far, far above them. It was enough light for them to make out the translucent walkway which would allow them to continue when the solid floor ended.

They followed the walkway cautiously. It was hard for them not to look down through the now translucent floor and see the huge void below, a void so deep that the shafts of light failed to illuminate the bottom. Other than the walkway, the chamber itself was largely vacant except for a few square structures near the centre that appeared to be floating in mid air, like bubbles caught in frozen water. After much more walking they eventually reached the far side of the chamber where an archway led to another chamber almost as immense.

Light streamed into this chamber much more than the last as large chunks of the roof appeared to be missing. Crossing this chamber was another suspended walkway,

Chapter 19: The Children Win

but what drew their eyes was what was located on either side of their path. Rows upon rows of clear cylindrical shaped containers stood on end on end. Each housed one or more strange creatures of various shapes and sizes. There were many banks of these containers arranged in rows, stacked high to the ceiling and stretched outwards into the far distance. Small walkways led off from the gangway which allowed them, if they chose, to get in and amongst the giant jars. However, some of the walkways looked to be in a very dangerous condition while others had collapsed entirely, breaking open some containers below. The missing sections of the roof had also taken their toll on the banks of jars, many were broken and smashed. The fate of the creatures within? Unknown.

Luke decided to venture down one of the creaky walkways, to get a better look at what was inside some of the still intact containers. Up close he could see that each row seemed to house many creatures of the same species, well at least they appeared to all look alike. The first row contained translucent jelly-like creatures, where nothing but their skeletons were visible. The next row contained a worm-like species except that these were four feet long and had wings. The third row contained creatures that Luke was now very familiar with, for these cylinders contained the creatures he and Aaron had fought on numerous occasions before, the so-called "Scavengers". He also noticed that several of the jars were broken and empty.

Surface

It was now obvious where these creatures had come from, but Aaron, who had joined Luke on the walkway, thought it still needed saying.

"So the children are responsible for the creatures?" Then, after a pause, Aaron voiced a darker thought. "The children made 'em, and now their twisted experiments have escaped, probably through those holes in the roof!" Aaron pointed upwards. He was perhaps jumping to conclusions, but out loud that thought almost made them both turn around and go home. Maybe delivering this relic was not a good idea. The mystery of who, or indeed what, these children were deepened.

Despite this, Luke was resolved to seeing this through and only made up his mind when he had all the information.

"Let's not hang around any more," Luke said. Aaron nodded before adding. "Let's be careful, as helping you return this relic may be one of the dumbest things I have ever done. This best be worth it!"

They walked on until they passed under another archway into a much smaller chamber. There appeared to be no way on from here, at least that was how it appeared to be until the floor de-materialised from underneath their very feet! They began falling; they accelerated like they did before in the elevator to Luke's home, only this time there

Chapter 19: The Children Win

were no brakes to save them. Frantically Aaron removed his rope from his pack. hoping to hook onto something, but the wind ripped it from his hand as they accelerated to terminal velocity. The floor was now in sight, and it was coming up fast.

The floor rushed up. They both blacked out but only for a second. An unknown force caused them to de-accelerate rapidly, bringing them to a stop just a few inches from the floor. They floated there, almost frozen with shock. An electronic hum of some kind, maybe a generator wound down in the background and they dropped the last few inches unceremoniously onto the metal tiled surface of the shaft's floor. What had stopped them they did not know, but they were thankful that it did. Aaron's rope too had been stopped, but gravity was now acting normally again and the rope that had been previously suspended high above them came tumbling down. The end of the rope cracked like a whip as it hit the floor while the trailing section draped itself over both of them.

Aaron removed the rope from a-top his head and repacked it. They then exited through the only doorway from the shaft, which led them into yet another massive chamber complete with more glass cylinders. However, unlike the ones in the last chamber these were all one size, all tall and slender approx 10ft high by 3ft wide. The creatures inside looked almost human, but their features were too obscured by the strange, dark liquid that

Surface

surrounded them.

"I think…" Aaron paused "I think I have had enough of this place. My heart cannot take this any more. Even if we do survive this, I will be dead by thirty from the stress!" Luke agreed, and he knew that with every step they took this was becoming more and more of a disaster as well as the concept being just a bad idea. Luke had almost been killed twice now in one day. He sighed. What else could they do? He doubted they could return the way they came.

They both noticed a dim light in the distance that could not be natural this far down. It was also noticeably warmer, even warmer than the creator outside; their clothes became damp with sweat.

"It's just over there," Luke pointed at the light.

But neither of them moved, their determination seemed drained. It was a strange and dangerous place, but that did not stop them from taking a rest, if only so they could calm themselves. They sat down with their backs against the archway, they only intended to rest for a few minutes. However, that was all it took for both of them to drift off to sleep. Exhaustion had taken its toll and the warm air comfortable.

Luke was holding Antheria by the hand as the pair of them walked along the beach in some unknown, yet also

Chapter 19: The Children Win

familiar land. There was a child with them, their child. Luke felt content, he had everything a man would need he was at peace here. He glanced happily at his son, who was merely skipping along the beach in front of them. He was a blond-haired boy no more than five years of age. Luke turned to kiss Antheria, but something made him look away, something made him look back at his son. The boy had stopped skipping. He was not just simply standing, no, he seemed frozen mid-skip as if he had run into a giant flypaper, practically levitating off of the sand. The child then turned on one foot which was still partially on the ground, as if he was a puppet suspended by strings. What stood facing them was not the face of Luke's son. No the face was wrong, not human. Luke's heart raced and began beating quickly like a drum.

Terrified he turned to Antheria, yet she was no longer there. The beach changed to stone, the sea grew cold and frozen, and the sky went dark. Then the thing that was his son spoke:

"Return what is ours," It demanded.

Luke awoke from the what he realised was a dream, likely brought on by the children. He felt resolved again for he knew the only way to be rid of these nightmares, both sleeping and waking, was to finish what he came here to do, to do what they demanded.

Surface

Somewhat rested now after an unknown time asleep, they picked themselves up, ignoring their complaining muscles when they stood. They began to make their way slowly along the walkway to the source of the light. The light was coming from a suspended room, not unlike the ones they witnessed floating in the ether in an earlier chamber. There appeared to be no way across as there was a gaping chasm between them and the room, that is until a walkway extended silently to bridge the gap. They made their way across to the suspended box. The box was completely transparent; a maze of walkways and conduits below were clearly visible through it.

Luke was starting to feel dizzy looking down, so he focused on the one solid object in the room, a circular podium that was bolted to the floor. The podium displayed various lights and lit symbols, the source of the light. As they both looked at it, the symbols seemed to shift and change as if some silent being was tracing its way through a book that was written in a strange, foreign tongue. In the middle of the reappearing and vanishing symbols was a recess, a recess that appeared to be the exact same shape and size as the relic that Luke carried. At last, he could be rid of it.

As they approached the console the recess began to glow, and the relic in Luke's pack hummed in response.

Luke was hesitant at first, but despite thinking about all he

Chapter 19: The Children Win

had been through he was still resolved to complete his task. He would finish this and hang the consequences. Before Aaron could even think about objecting, Luke removed the relic from his burnt pack and then placed it into the recess; it slid slowly into the depression. The console too began to hum softly and glowed more brightly.

Aaron let out a gasp. He stood there pointing with a working finger at the misty shapes that had begun to form around the console in front of them. Slowly the shapes gained form, until there were seven children standing in a semi-circle in front of them. All the children appeared to be smiling, all except one of them.

The children bowed and in hushed tones they each thanked Luke one by one, for what he had done; they seemed to ignore Aaron completely. The last child, however, remained silent.

It was not clear at first, but the children's skin seemed to be paler then Luke remembered. Not only that, they also seemed taller than before. The children continued to change, they now grew more slender and their limbs grew longer. This continued more noticeably until their limbs were now twice the length of a normal adult human, let alone a child. The children were no longer children, they had changed into something else, something strange. They stood some eight feet tall, the skin of these beings had

Surface

changed from pale grey to white and, what's more, the skin was radiating light, glowing like sunlight. Their features were indistinct due to the glow, all that is except the brighter pale blue light from their eyes.

"See us now, in our true forms" they spoke together, "for you will be the last of your kind to see us." That sounded like a threat, Luke and Aaron both thought.

"We graciously thank you for the return of what you have come to know as the relics. We apologise for deceiving you with our appearance, we only appeared as children after observing your culture. We hoped that this form of innocence would make your kind more responsive."

"Why did you put us through all this? Why do you need this? Answer me," Luke demanded almost too harshly.

The tallest of them replied to this question alone:

"You have returned the core… relic, so we owe you answers. We did not intend to cause you distress, we could not help the obstacles in the way. The technology here is erratic without the core and is not designed with your species in mind. Your journey here was necessary, as was ours. Like you we wish not to be here at all."

"And my second question?" Luke asked with a rather condescending tone.

Chapter 19: The Children Win

"It is most likely beyond your comprehension, but we will endeavour to answer in as simplistic terms as possible. To put it basically, the relic you hold there is a power source of compressed changeable matter. The energy it produces almost never expires as it taps into multiple-dimensions, worlds that are not here but at the time same are. The core you call the relic combines the energies of those worlds into one focal point, producing almost limitless energy."

"If that is a simple explanation, then I do not want to hear the complicated one." Aaron blurted out. The creatures continued to completely ignore Aaron as though he was not there, could they not hear him?

"When the core was exposed to certain forces, such as those generated in a severe impact, it fractured sending its shards over vast distances. The shattering also opened tears in the fabric of space time, opening up unstable portals to various universes. At first we sought to contain the creatures that burst forth from those tears; however, we were overwhelmed without the power of the core. We were forced to rely on more primitive and far less effective power sources, so were unable to contain them all; it only took a breeding pair of each to spread out amongst your world.

The tears themselves have mainly mended naturally now, all except for a few, which includes the one you entered

Surface

by."

"Entered by? So we are not in our world?," Luke asked.

"You are correct, the place you reside is not of your universe, it is the one we are trapped in. This allows us to easily appear to you. With the core restored the remaining tears will be healed, so that you and us will re-emerge in in the correct universe once again."

"So we can go home?," Aaron asked and Luke repeated.

"If you so wish," the being responded.

"So this is where the creatures came from, they come from this dimension?" Luke said in an attempt to understand and continued, "I take it that these shards are the relics that myself and others have collected over many years. So why did they all look like mundane items such as hammers and chalices?," Luke inquired, almost relentless in his questioning.

"This is indeed perplexing and even we are not sure how this has occurred. Our best estimation is that the shards latched onto your dimension and took on the shapes of near-by items. Perhaps this was in order to prevent it from being split infinitely and converted into pure energy. If that were to happen, there would be a reaction strong enough to vaporise this entire galaxy in every universe the

Chapter 19: The Children Win

relic had connected to. However, now that it is combined again, the core is now stable."

Luke glanced fearfully at the relic, and Aaron was visibly shocked at the power of the core. Destroying a galaxy was certainly something he could understand.

"You mentioned an impact?"

"Yes, an impact with this craft and your planet's surface, brought about by your sun's unstable activity. A solar flare generated by a massive solar event, struck your planet and us while we were in orbit at the time."

"So you are aliens? Were you observing? Why...?" Luke was interrupted.

"To see if it was inhabitable," the aliens replied. Although the creatures were lacking in human facial features, Luke could still tell that the aliens were becoming irritated. What he was sure of now was that he angry again, no, fuming!

"Inhabitable! You were going to conquer us!?" Luke yelled. He started to reach for the core he had inserted, perhaps to undo what he had done.

"You misunderstand, part of our survey requirements requires that there is no pre-existing sentient life on the

Surface

planet. We only seek a new and uninhabited world in which to call our home. We were about to leave to find another." The aliens despite being featureless somehow seemed to look somewhat sadder.

"Our home was destroyed," they then said in unison.

Despite not being sure whether believe them or not, Luke still felt sorry for the aliens, and he calmed down and backed away from the relic again.

Luke pondered carefully on what to ask next. He had so many other questions he wanted answered, such as why he was chosen, and why the children appeared to him the most above everyone else. But in the end he asked a different question, a question that he thought was probably a stupid question with an obvious answer.

"So what will happen now that I have returned this to you?"

To this question they all answered in unison.

"With this core we will wake, with this core we will leave."

"Good, they will leave", Aaron thought. He was glad of it, he felt better about going along with Luke and letting the children have the core, perhaps this was the right thing to do after all.

Chapter 19: The Children Win

The relic began to hum louder now and the floor began to vibrate slightly before stabilising again. The chamber around their bubble room lit up, exposing even more and stranger architecture.

It was at this point that Luke remembered what he had learned back in the monk's library. He remembered that the children were responsible for leading people out onto the surface, so he wondered why they had done this. He put this question to them. This turned out be the most important question he would ask.

"We needed your species' help and the only way to gain your assistance was to assist your people in turn. We studied you for the first ten solar cycles and realised that your species could not survive on the frigid surface long enough to return to us the fragments."

To that end we used what was left of our energies to penetrate deep into your planet's crust and then we released billions of tons of carbon dioxide into your atmosphere, while providing us with basic power. The carbon would trap the heat within your planet's atmosphere and cause temperatures to increase. Once your planet was again inhabitable for your species, we made contact telekineticly. It was then just a matter of convincing your species' to gather the shards. Unfortunately, we did not take into account your species'

Surface

capacity for greed, fear and anger. It seemed that your species would much rather kill each other than help us. We had to adapt, learn, develop, so we learned your methods and resorted to trickery where we exploited one of your species' greatest traits – greed, greed for relics of power."

"In the end it took us over two hundred and fifty cycles of your sun to gather all the fragments, yours being the last. We regret using these methods, but now that we have the completed core we will leave. Our false interference will be at an end, and the carbon release will stop."

Aaron picked up on this last point, when Luke did not. Even though Aaron was not scientifically minded in the slightest, he understood the basic point that the carbon release was what warmed the planet, so logically he knew what would happen once it stopped.

"The release will stop? But won't that make everything cold again?," Aaron questioned the aliens. The aliens ignored Aaron, but Luke too wanted to know, so he repeated the question for him.

"This is regrettable but necessary. Once we leave our artificial influence will leave with us. Your planet will return to its original state, its correct state, a state we should never have interfered with in the first place. It will be as we promised to you relic-seekers, your world will be

Chapter 19: The Children Win

restored within twenty rotations of your planet around the sun."

Aaron's relief at thinking he had let Luke do the right thing was now well and truly squashed.

"Restored!? You will kill everyone on the surface and make it uninhabitable!," Aaron shouted out in anger.

Surprisingly, the children did answer. "Your planet will warm naturally in five hundred cycles as the solar activity of your star normalises. Your species as a whole will likely survive as it did before, underground."

Luke had compassion for the aliens' plight, but that did not stop him reaching for the relic, to remove it from the console. He felt the relic vibrate as it began to hum even louder. Before he could begin to pull, the ship shifted violently to the left, knocking him off balance. Once he was steady again on his feet and reached out once more, but this time he paused. There was a voice at the back of his mind, it was telling him, that he should just let it happen. Maybe all the things he had been forced to endure, the psychological and psychical scars, just made him want to give in to this voice. The surface world was not worth saving. It was a savage place, the aliens meant no harm. This line of thought triggered images of past bloody battles that he hoped now lay dormant asserted themselves in his mind.

Surface

The aliens sensed this, and before long their voices joined the ones already present in the back of his mind.

"They murdered your people, this will be justice," one whispered

"The world will be made anew" another one whispered.

"Please, do not doom us, to be trapped forever", a final voice pleaded.

Luke found that these points were valid, how many people had he met who had tried to kill him or at least each other?

A dark thought outgrew the rest. "Maybe they do deserve it..."

"All the children have done is help us. Do they deserve not to be set free?," Luke reasoned, his thoughts going in one direction now.

"They did haunt me but at least I will be rid of them this way." Luke shouted from within his head.

"Well, what are you waiting for, an invitation? Pull the darn thing out already," Aaron screamed at Luke, briefly snapping him out of it.

Chapter 19: The Children Win

"Why?," Luke said simply.

"What do you mean why? Did you not hear what I said? Everyone will die!" Aaron screamed in frustration.

"Everyone up here will die," Luke corrected, before voicing his thoughts out loud now.

"Does this world not deserve it? I mean look what happened to us, happened to me." Luke's eye's widened. "Worse, I have become like one of those savages. Remember the battle? I killed a man!"

"So you're going to make amends for that by killing everyone else? What about Geal, the monks...?" He paused, "What about me? You know they will never allow me to stay in your home." Luke knew he owed Aaron a lot and would do all that he could to make sure Aaron could live with his people, but he still did not remove the core.

Seeing that his words had failed, Aaron tried to make a grab for the relic, but as he approached the children finally noticed him and a energy barrier immediately appeared and separated him from both Luke and the console. Aaron took the last path open to him and continued his verbal attack.

"Do you want to live like a prisoner all your life? Antheria told me what your life was like down there. Nothing is ever private, you only do what you are told to do. If you deviate you are chucked out." This did make Luke flinch a little. He remembered that he had originally set out to free himself and perhaps find something help to free his people. This would have the opposite effect. He would be trapped again, forever.

"What about Antheria? Would she want to be part of this… genocide?," Aaron added as a last remark. That remark turned out to be just what was needed. Luke knew now that Aaron was right. He could not go through with it, for he remembered the guilt he felt even back at the bandit's camp when the Over King had a man executed in his place. He tried to imagine that guilt magnified a million times over, and then he realised that Antheria would also experience that guilt, for the part she had played in it all.

Aaron stared at Luke as Luke's hands reached for the relic once more. The aliens reacted and one of them even tried to reach for Luke's hand, but instead it simply passed through him. Of course, these aliens were still mere projections. They had no physical forms, except maybe those in the cylinders.

"This world must come first!" Luke screamed, resolute now, he began to remove the relic, even though he knew he would be condemning the aliens to be trapped forever,

Chapter 19: The Children Win

in place of his people. No doubt, whatever his choice it would likely haunt him for forever more.

He pulled harder on the relic, it was not going to come easily. The aliens screamed directly into his head, begging and shouting at him to stop. Now the familiar drum roll started up in his head faster and louder than it had ever before, accompanying the shouts and screams.

His vision blurred and his nose began to bleed, yet he continued to pull. The relic shifted slightly. A sharp pain shot through his chest, and the drum roll became a jumbled mess. His heart was failing and his brain felt as if it was boiling, yet he still continued to pull.

The lights began to darken, and the ship lurched violently, perhaps slipping back into its original position. The relic, however, was coming loose. His arms failed him and he began to slump over the console his vision was now almost entirely gone as his consciousness faded. He had almost gotten the relic out if just had a little more strength. He could pull no more, his breath was leaving him. He felt a tug on his arms. It was Aaron, the barrier had fallen to allow him through. With Aaron's might added to his they both heaved upon the relic, all the time the aliens stepping up their mental attack on Luke's body and mind. Aaron's head too was pounding, he was not immune to the mental assault but was far less susceptible than Luke was. Then the relic finally came free. The ship

Surface was plunged into darkness, and Luke's world ceased to be.

"We've done it!" Aaron cheered.

Despite the pain, he could not help but to feel a tremendous sense of accomplishment that he had stopped this potential disaster.

His celebration was brief, however, as he witnessed Luke's lifeless body drop onto the cold floor. Despite Luke almost making the worst decision imaginable in Aaron's eyes, he was still his friend, so a great feeling of concern and fear for Luke's safety overwhelmed him. A tear even began to roll down his cheek.

Dizzy and distraught, Aaron dropped to the floor and dragged himself over to Luke's side. Luke lay there motionless. The colour had drained from his face.

He looked up and shouted to the aliens, "What have you done to him?"

There was no reply instead the aliens faded Their mission had failed for now at least until another could be recruited

Aaron examined Luke. He vainly hoped that what the effects of what aliens had done him were temporary, but he could tell immediately that this was not the case. Luke appeared to be injured internally as there was blood

Chapter 19: The Children Win

streaming from his nose, ears and mouth. Aaron listened for Luke's breath, there was none. This was beyond Aaron, he could not bring people back he nor did he know of any method to do so. He was helpless to aid him. He let out a uncontrollable cry before stealing him self again. "Not leaving you here, mate," he said to Luke's body.

All of the aliens by now had faded, all that is except one. This last alien had changed its form back into that of a human, a small ginger-haired boy. This was the same boy that, Luke had seen after the battle at Whitevale. The boy pointed up to the top left of the console that once held the relic. As if at the boy's direction, a button raised it self seemingly from nothing on the console, inviting Aaron to press it. The boy then said in a normal child-like voice, "Forever slumber."

Aaron did not trust him, but now with the relic removed, what harm could it do? Aaron hit the control and hoped. All the remaining lights extinguished themselves and the image of the boy flickered before vanishing. The ship shut down along with the alien's connection to the outside world, now presumably severed. The button then slowly receded into the console, but it remained lit. It pulsed as if inviting to be pushed again, to start this nightmare anew.

Aaron returned to his dead friend and heaved him onto his shoulder. He was still warm to the touch, his body heat had not yet drained away. Aaron slowly made his way

Surface

along the dark gangways and corridors with only torch light for comfort, that and the light from the cylinders that seemed to still to be functioning. The creatures inside were still and dormant. He entered the bottom of the shaft that they had originally dropped down from and realised he was trapped. He looked up and doubted it would be possible to climb it.

Distraught, he placed his dead friend down onto the floor. Luke's body appeared to glow gently, so Aaron carefully moved Luke from where he had placed him only to find a ray of hope. A tile dimly glowed in the centre of shaft's floor. Aaron touched it and for some emergency protocol kicked in. Slowly but surely the floor began to rise silently as if on a cushion of air.

At the top Aaron once more placed his dead friend back onto his shoulder. He planned to take him away from this place, so he could at least offer him a proper burial.

The ship seemed to go on forever, each step was agony. Aaron was not sure he would be able to carry Luke for much further, longer or even get him self out and down the mountain.

Aaron felt a light, moist breeze on his right shoulder, "Where is this coming from?" he wondered.
No, it was Luke's breath. He was alive!

Chapter 19: The Children Win

Aaron set him down and tried to wake him, but Luke remained unresponsive. Knowing he was not dead spurred Aaron on and gave him that last bit of energy needed to try and get himself and Luke out of this place. They couldn't be far from the exit. He was about to pick Luke up again when he spotted something out of the corner of his eye. There was something in front of them, a light, and from the shadow of that light a figure was silhouetted on the wall from around a corner. Someone or something was approaching. Aaron searched for a weapon. He spotted a metal bar lying on the floor amongst roof debris. He picked it up and held it out in front of him, ready to face what ever horror approached.

He silently moved along the gangway and into a short corridor. He reached the corner in the corridor and waited. He could hear footsteps. When he was sure they were close enough he jumped around the corner brandishing his weapon; he roared and brought the piece of metal down on his target, only to stop it a few inches from Antheria's head.

"Hey," she said nervously as Aaron lowered his weapon.

"Hey," Aaron said back, weakly.

"You know I could have killed you," Aaron said, finally.

"I had to come," was the only reply.

Surface

She then circled around Aaron as if inspecting him. Aaron noticed that her ankle seemed to have noticeably improved, he guessed it was not as bad as they had first thought.

"Luke...,"
Aaron stumbled for words "Luke is...?" Dead? Hurt? Dying? He was not certain. He did not want to upset her too much so he decided to go with he was hurt, however before he finished his sentence he was interrupted by a tug on his backpack as Antheria opened it.

"Aaron?," she asked "Why have you still got the relic?"

Aaron thought it was strange that she was more concerned about the relic than Luke. Did she not wonder where Luke was? There was a sound, a familiar sound the sound of a sharp metal blade being taken from a leather sheaf. Aaron once again had a blade at his throat! He looked down, it was his blade. She must have picked it up from where he had left it at the entrance, the barrier of darkness barrier presumably gone, the relic had repaired the tears.

"Well, I always liked a bit of foreplay, but I normally draw the line at blades." Aaron said.

"Funny, Aaron, as always." she said sarcastically.

Chapter 19: The Children Win

"I need the relic so I can finish your mission." She said

"Easy there, you need to know why we abandoned this quest," Aaron said calmly.

"I can guess, is it because doing it will bring back the ice? Am I on the right lines?," she asked.

"She knows, how? She too will doom everyone and ... my family?," Aaron thought to himself.

"What is it with you people and wanting to end the world!?," Aaron shouted losing his calm. Antheria remained silent, but tightened her grip.

With her free hand, she removed the relic from the back pack and held it under her arm. She was about to release Aaron but then paused, a thought had struck her.

"Where is Luke?"

"So you finally want to know. Funny I would have thought that would have been your first question." Aaron decided to change his answer from the one he was going to give earlier. Maybe if she thought that Luke had died trying to stop this madness, then perhaps she could be swayed like Luke was and then leave this place.

Surface

Aaron gestured around the corner. Cautiously with blade drawn Antheria moved away from Aaron and rounded the corner. It was then when she noticed Luke, he was pale and motionless. She lowered her blade and ran to him.

"Luke, Luke!!? I am doing this for us, please don't be ... is he?" she asked Aaron

"He is," Aaron lied. He held out his hand for her to return the relic.

She batted it away "NO! I will make his death mean something, I will finish what he started," she screamed and then directed the knife towards Aaron's throat once more.

"He died trying to stop this," Aaron bellowed. "Why do you want to destroy us all?"

"Why? WHY!? Let me tell you why. I learned something you see, I know this is necessary even if Luke did not believe it in the end." She began to explain what had happened all that time ago when she had followed Luke to the surface…

Chapter 20: The Fate of the Sphere

I had escaped to the surface. I glanced back at the hole from which I had emerged, the sounds of my pursuers were growing louder. Desperately I ran down the hill towards the track I could see below, hoping to follow it into the forest beyond.

I did mange to make it to the track successfully, but unfortunately I ran straight into a hooded and masked Hammerite, who I presume had just emerged from the main entrance.

Before I could turn and flee, the Hammerite tackled me, an arm rounded on my throat. At that moment I honestly thought I would be strangled. The pressure was thankfully released slightly, but new pressure was applied to my wrists as my hands were bound together. After making sure I was secure, the Hammerite ,who I presumed to be a man released my throat and began pulling on my restraints. I then was dragged up the path and into the open entrance tunnel.

Unexpectedly, instead of heading straight to the lift, he stopped just a few feet inside. From behind I heard a click as a concealed button had presumably been pressed. A door squeaked and creaked open, allowing us access to a small hidden room to the side. It may once have been a

Surface

room of some importance, but now all that it seemed to contain was the decaying remains of now illegible papers and their destroyed containers.

He carefully closed the door behind us, snuffing out almost all light , and I began to panic, wondering what he might do. Then there was click in the darkness as a torch was turned on. The torch was then placed on an old table in the centre of the room. By the pointing of his finger I was directed to sit down on a chair that was in remarkably good condition when compared to everything else in the room.

The Hammerite circled the table to the other side, where there was no other chair, so he remained standing. The Hammerite removed his hood. I could not believe it, it was Jason, I knew him well, but I never knew he was a Hammerite or had it in him to be one.

"Has anyone seen you?," he asked in a strangely panicky voice.

"No," I said, as my heart began to slowly calm.

"Thank the children, if they had.…. I would not like to think about what they would have done to you. What made you decide to go out there into this savage world?," he asked seemingly genuinely puzzled.

Chapter 20: The Fate of the Sphere

"To find Luke," I replied, as if the answer should be obvious. Jason's face dropped at this remark. Maybe it was because he disliked Luke, as Luke was always breaking the rules, or maybe it was because I seemed to spend so much time with Luke, and Jason felt I should have spent that time with him.

"You should not have come after him," he said bluntly.

I was starting to get angry, what right did he have to govern my life? I must have been visibly displeased as Jason seemed to refine his statement, most likely in an effort not to seem so overly hostile.

"What I meant to say is that this world out here is a dangerous and hostile place. You could be easily killed out here."

Was he genuinely concerned? I was not sure whether to believe him or not. To me, this world seemed like paradise, compared to home, so I thought it was another Hammerite lie. But then I thought, this is Jason. Would he lie about this? Well he did lied about being a Hammerite.

So I effectively told him he was a liar. "No, that is not true. This place is beautiful. No, I think the real situation is that this place is paradise and you Hammers want to keep it to yourselves and have your own private garden of Eden. Is that it?"

Surface

"I speak the truth, there is a reason why we still live underground" Jason replied.

"Let me tell you a story", he began ,as he explained the true history of my people and the savagery that had befallen us at the hands of what he called t"he non-believers". He explained to me in explicit detail how we were almost wiped out by your people, Aaron. He said that our underground home and the few sanctuaries dotted about on the surface were all that was left. Staying below, away from the savage world, was our only hope at survival, until the one day when we might discover a way to fight back. Jason said that day had come.

Aaron was not shocked by this news he already knew the dark history of his people. It was partially out of this guilt for what his people had done that caused him to choose to remain with Luke through thick and thin.

I was shaken by the story, I feared even more now for Luke's safety. So much so well ,I burst into tears. Luke would not survive sin uch a place.

Jason did take pity on me, he knew I truly cared for Luke. But the reason for this would continue to elude Jason, even to this very day.

"I will let you into a secret about Luke and I promise you

Chapter 20: The Fate of the Sphere

he will be okay, if you will do something for me. Well, not just for me but for all of our people."

I was hesitant, I did not want agree to whatever this was straight away without knowing what price I would have to pay. I asked for more details.

"No strings," Jason said in reply. "All I want is for you to help Luke when he returns, just make sure he does not fail. I want nothing more than that. Keep him safe, deal?"

How could I not accept? I ,of course, wanted to keep him safe. I nodded my head in acceptance, but I still wanted further details.

"Well, you know how I said one day we would fight back...?" *Jason explained about Luke's destiny, how it was him who was destined to return the relic. Jason also explained what returning the relic would do to the world and how it would allow the people of the colony to start anew.*

"But that's murder," *I cried.* "It would make us no better than the aliens, Luke would never go along with this."

"He currently does not know that this will happen," *Jason said quietly, as though Luke could be listening.* "It would be your job to ensure that, even if he does find out, he must still completes his mission."

Surface

"Think about" it, he said, "Is it any more than what they deserve? With those people still out there, we could never hope to return, but in a few years when the planet warms again we can take back what is ours."

Aaron scoffed at this part of the story. Did she genuinely think that the world would re-warm in a few years? No, it would be centuries. The childr... aliens said so themselves. He could tell Antheria the truth, but doubted she would believe him, so Antheria continued her story.

"Are you listening Aaron?" she said, irritated. Aaron nodded.

"Where was I? Ah yes"... *after telling me the consequences he then made sure I would go along with him with the words. "If you do not ensure Luke finishes his mission, then he will likely die."*

Reluctantly I agreed almost too formally, as I entered into this verbal contract, a contract I intend not to break. Jason said. "I will tell the other Hammerites. When Luke returns he will not be harmed, but he will have to leave once more. It is at that time, you must go with him. What ever happens he must not fail. Come now, I will sneak you back in through another entrance. I will then contact you again in a few days time. It's best that you do not go back to your regular job, there is room in my block in the

Chapter 20: The Fate of the Sphere

upper district."

"After that we became more friendly, and he taught me a lot about this savage world, about you and your people," she said while brandishing the knife wildly at Aaron.

"I can only presume if you had not turned up, like the brigand you are, Luke would have finished his quest and my people would be free. Now give me the relic!," Antheria once again demanded.

Aaron stood fast

"So you were the backup, then, should Luke fail? Yes, the children had it all planned out, didn't they?," he said rhetorically and went on to say, "I know what this is. This is simply revenge, revenge for what was done to your people two hundred years ago! Don't you see? The aliens have manipulated you and Luke all along, so they could set themselves free using ancient grudges as their levering point. I am glad I stopped Luke, and glad that Luke himself had the wisdom in the end to realise what he was doing was just plain wrong! Yes, the aliens killed 'im for it, but he died a hero's death."

Antheria knew Aaron had a point. Two hundred years is a long time to hold a grudge, but this thought was snuffed out, snuffed out by pure rage, rage at the thought of what would have happened if Aaron had not stopped Luke.

Surface

Luke would still be alive. She was also felt indignation for herself for failing the most important part of her mission, which was to keep Luke safe. She realised that she should not have stayed behind. She had intended to follow them so that she could take the relic from them should they fail, but the barrier stopped her. She knew she should have been with Luke. Her grip on the bladed weapon tightened and she was visibly shaking. Aaron could see this and began to step back slowly. Was he going for a weapon?

Her anger and rage reached a crescendo, and it was all directed at Aaron. She lunged at him. Aaron dodged this attack, barely, as his clothing, and some flesh were torn. Aaron had dropped his weapon earlier when Antheria first attacked, so he had no means of defending himself. But he had an idea, one chance. After dodging a second thrust that he was more ready for, Aaron used his cat-like reflexes to jump back, putting some distance between them. He used the time this brought to remove the relic from the top of his pack. He then threw it down the walkway, knowing Antheria would have to drop her weapon if she wanted to catch it.

Antheria did indeed drop the blade and caught the relic elegantly. She did not stop, she ran down the walkway to the centre of the alien ship. Now that the blade was no longer at Aaron's throat he could act, so he ran after her. He didn't know where his energy came from, but he was able to catch up quickly with Antheria. He made a dive for

Chapter 20: The Fate of the Sphere

her legs. She went flying further than Aaron would have thought, further than Luke had with the chalice months earlier, except this time, Antheria crashed not into a wall but into the railings guarding the walkway.

Two centuries or so of decay takes its toll even on alien materials, and the railing gave way to the force of Antheria's body crashing into it. She now dangled there by only one hand from what remained of the railing, the relic sphere held in her other hand resting against her leg, all of which was hanging over the void.

She could see Luke down the walkway as Aaron rushed over towards her. "He died to stop this," she thought. Aaron neared. His hand was out stretched. "He's trying to save me after what I did?," she thought to herself. She saw Luke's eyes flicker, he was not dead. She had to live, he would not want this. "Drop the relic and give me your hand," Aaron shouted. It was too late, the railing gave way. Aaron tried to catch her, but she was already out of reach. Antheria and the relic tumbled into the abyss.

Her screams went quiet, she was either out of earshot or had hit the bottom. Aaron dropped to his knees, distraught by his failure to save her, just as Luke opened his eyes. Aaron knew that Luke would no doubt panic when he found that Antheria had gone missing from the cave, and that he would no doubt ask Aaron what he knew. But Aaron would claim to know nothing. He would never tell

Surface

Luke the truth about what had happened. Who knows what Luke would do if he found out. Secrets like these, however, have their way of coming to the surface.

Printed in Great Britain
by Amazon